"Is something wrong?"

Seth couldn't look at Trina for fear the hole in his heart would grow bigger and swallow him up. "I'm sorry, Trina. I shouldn't have and I'm sorry."

"Shouldn't have what?" she asked.

Was she being coy? Or hadn't she felt what he felt? No, he couldn't believe that, even if she was going to make him say it aloud.

"I'm sorry for what happened yesterday. I promise you it won't ever happen again."

Trina stumbled backward as if she'd been struck and her mouth fell open. In the dimming light he noticed her cheeks suddenly glistened with tears.

"I understand, Seth, why you and I can never be... I understand that you're Amish and I'm *Englisch*. But I'm not sorry about the affection you've shown me. And I'm not sorry you know I feel the same way about you."

Watching her dash back toward her house, Seth fought the impulse to follow her and profess his affection—his *love*—too.

Letting her go was the most difficult thing he'd ever done...

Carrie Lighte lives in Massachusetts, where her neighbors include several Mennonite farming families. She loves traveling and first learned about Amish culture when she visited Lancaster County, Pennsylvania, as a young girl. When she isn't writing or reading, she enjoys baking bread, playing word games and hiking, but her all-time favorite activity is bodyboarding with her loved ones when the surf's up at Coast Guard Beach on Cape Cod.

Books by Carrie Lighte

Love Inspired

Amish Country Courtships

Amish Triplets for Christmas
Anna's Forgotten Fiancé
An Amish Holiday Wedding
Minding the Amish Baby
Her New Amish Family

Visit the Author Profile page at Harlequin.com.

Her New Amish Family

Carrie Lighte

HARLEQUIN® LOVE INSPIRED®

Recycling programs
for this product may
not exist in your area.

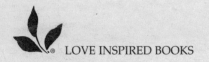 LOVE INSPIRED BOOKS

ISBN-13: 978-1-335-53916-8

Her New Amish Family

Printed in U.S.A.

And be ye kind one to another,
tenderhearted, forgiving one another,
even as God for Christ's sake hath forgiven you.
—*Ephesians* 4:32

For mothers and mother figures everywhere,
with special thanks to L.D. and S.D.
for their help.

Chapter One

Trina Smith expected to find a gas stove in the little Amish house, but the refrigerator surprised her. She hadn't considered a fridge could be powered by gas, too. Not that she had much use for either appliance; Trina lost her appetite when her mother, Patience, died six months ago of leukemia. When Trina did eat, it was only to nibble a piece of toast or an apple, and even then she had to force herself to swallow. Just like she had to force herself to go to bed at night and then to rise in the morning. She was going through the motions because nothing seemed to come naturally anymore.

She set her suitcase down on the floor of the tiny kitchen. Although no one else was in the house, she tiptoed into the parlor. From the dark braided rug to the gas lamp to the sparse furniture, the room was exactly as her mother had described, right down to the ticktock of the clock on the wall.

"As loudly as that clock marked off the seconds, I felt like time was standing still," her mother once said. "I think it was the clock that made me realize nothing would ever change unless I changed it for myself."

And so, when she'd turned eighteen, Patience had left the little house. She left the Amish community in Willow Creek, Pennsylvania. And, most significantly, she left her family, which by that time consisted only of her austere, indifferent, drunkard father, Abe Kauffman. Now Patience's daughter was returning in her place.

Trina walked down the hallway with its bare wooden floor and opened the door to a back room. This would have been where Abe slept. Trina quickly closed the door again. She peeked into the other bedroom, her mother's girlhood room. It was furnished with a wooden chair, a plain dresser and a bed covered with a quilt that reminded Trina of those her mother had stitched for both of them to use in their own house. Trina remembered how, toward the end of her mother's illness, no amount of blankets could keep Patience warm.

Trina shivered and walked back to the kitchen, hoping to find a canister of coffee or tea. The first cupboard she opened contained neatly stacked rows of white dishes. The second held glasses and mugs. The third was empty except for a small gray mouse that scurried to the back corner where it squeezed through a crack.

"Ack!" Trina yelped and slammed the cupboard door.

"What's wrong?" someone asked from behind.

Trina shouted, "Ack!" a second time. Whirling around, she saw a short, plump, white-haired woman wearing glasses and traditional Amish attire.

Squinting, the woman repeated, "What's the matter?"

"I-I saw a mouse," Trina stuttered. "It startled me."

"I dare say you startled it, too," the woman said with a chuckle and set the basket she was carrying on the table. "I'm Martha Helmuth. I live next door. You must be Trina?"

Martha Helmuth—of course! Trina's mother had often said she would have run away long before she turned eighteen if it weren't for Martha Helmuth, whose door and arms were always open whenever Patience needed a place to escape to or someone to embrace her.

"Yes, I'm Trina. Trina Smith," she confirmed,

wondering how Martha knew her name, as her mother hadn't been in contact with anyone from Willow Creek since Trina was born twenty-five years ago.

"*Wilkom* to your home, Trina," the woman said warmly. "The *Englisch* attorney told us you wouldn't arrive until the first of March on Tuesday. I would have stocked the cupboards with staples yesterday if I had known you'd be here today. I hope you don't mind I held on to Abe's spare key. I've been trying to clean up the place for you."

"*Denki,*" Trina said, automatically using one of the many *Pennslyfaanisch Deitsch* words her mother had taught her. "That's very thoughtful of you."

"My, don't you sound just like your *mamm,*" Martha replied. "*Kumme* closer, so I can get a better look at you. My eyesight isn't what it used to be."

Trina obediently took a step toward Martha, who reached out and clasped Trina's hands in her own, squinting upward. Ordinarily Trina would have felt too self-conscious to allow a stranger to scrutinize her like this, but knowing how loving Martha had been to her mother, Trina was completely at ease in her presence.

"You're tall, *jah*? And you're a brunette, too.

That means your eyes must be blue like your *mamm*'s, as well?"

"*Neh*, they're green like my *daed*'s." Trina immediately regretted mentioning her *Englisch* father, Richard Smith, who'd divorced her mother while she was pregnant with Trina. He'd promised to see Trina, but aside from visiting briefly one Christmas or sending an occasional belated birthday card, he rarely kept in touch. And although he became a successful property developer, he'd never contributed financially to Trina's care; she and her mother had lived in near poverty for most of Trina's childhood. She hadn't even known how to contact him when her mother died. Not that he would have come to the funeral, but Trina thought he should at least have been informed his ex-wife had passed away. She hoped Martha wouldn't ask questions about him.

But the woman just clucked her tongue and said, "I can't get over how much you sound like Patience. Can you sing as beautifully as she did, too?"

Trina was surprised by Martha's praise. The Amish rarely complimented someone's singing voice lest she become proud about her abilities, which were a gift from the Lord. Yet she was pleased the older woman remembered this trait about her mother. Patience had taught Trina several songs from the Amish hymnal, the *Ausbund.* They were sung in German, a language her mother also made sure Trina knew as part of her homeschooling.

"*Neh*, no one has a voice like hers," Trina answered more wistfully than boastfully.

Martha's sunny countenance clouded when she murmured, "I was so sorry to hear of your *mamm*'s passing."

Moved by the sincerity in Martha's voice, Trina blinked back tears. *"Denki."*

Then Martha said, "We heard you were a schoolteacher."

"A preschool teacher, yes," Trina replied, figuring the *Englisch* attorney managing her grandfather's estate must have told Martha she was a teacher. Rather, she *used* to teach preschool until her mother became ill. Then Trina took a semester off to be with her mother as she went through chemotherapy. After Patience died, Trina was so devastated she could hardly take care of herself, much less manage a classroom of rambunctious preschoolers, and she lost her job.

Trina had depleted her savings account helping cover her mother's medical expenses, and she'd racked up a substantial amount of debt, too. For the past four months, she had been living off her credit card. If she hadn't been so impoverished, she never would have come to Willow Creek to claim the inheritance her grandfather bequeathed her. She figured the money she'd receive from selling his house would repay the debt Trina incurred from her mother's hospital bills. It wasn't for her own sake she wanted the restitution, but for her mother's. *Patience's father owed her at least that much.*

For some reason the attorney couldn't explain, Abe Kauffman had attached an odd condition to Trina's inheritance: she had to live in the house for two full months before it would be hers to sell. Otherwise, ownership would go to the Amish *leit* in Willow Creek. Trina suspected the stipulation was her grandfather's way of making a point, but she could only guess what that point might be. Was he trying to punish her somehow because her mother left the Amish? Did he think Trina would be so intimidated by the prospect of living there she'd automatically forfeit the house? If so, he underestimated her determination as well as how desperate her situation had become.

She had no idea how she was going to pay for groceries and other necessities, but at least for now she had a place to live. Her mother had told her Main Street was within walking distance. Maybe there was an *Englisch* business owner in need of temporary help. Trina was certain she'd find a way to earn an income. As challenging as her financial and life circumstances had often been, she relied on the Lord to sustain her. Even during her mother's illness and subsequent death, God had faithfully carried—was *still* faithfully carrying—Trina through her grief. Surely if He could help her survive that kind of loss, He would provide a way for her to earn enough money to cover her living expenses.

"It must have been difficult for you to leave your friends and job to *kumme* here," Martha said. To Trina's delight, the older woman pulled tea and honey from the basket.

"Mmm." Trina's boyfriend had broken up with her around the time her mother got sick, and Trina had spent so much time at the hospital with her mother she'd lost touch with the other teachers from school and acquaintances from church.

"Well, we're glad to have you as our neighbor now," Martha said. "As for that mouse, I'll ask my *groosskin*, Seth, to see what he can do. Seth and his *kinner*, Timothy and Tanner, moved to Willow Creek from Ohio when Seth's wife died. Now they live next door with me."

"Oh, no need to bother him," Trina said.

While she was grateful for the offer, she didn't want anyone else visiting her. She and her mother had managed without a man in the house for Trina's entire life. She didn't need one helping her now, especially not an Amish man.

When Seth and his sons returned from hiking along the creek that ran behind their yard and found their house empty, Seth's first impulse was to panic. *What's happened to* Groossmammi? Then he remembered she said she was taking a few items to Abe Kauffman's old house for his granddaughter. Martha had already put fresh sheets on the beds and linens in the washroom, but she wanted to make sure everything else was clean and in place.

Personally, Seth thought Martha was getting too involved, acting as if she were preparing a homecoming for one of her own relatives, of which there were few still surviving. Yes, Martha had gotten to know Abe well in the past few years since he quit drinking. And, yes, she'd told Seth she had loved the young Patience Kauffman like a daughter. But it bothered him she was going to all this trouble for an *Englischer* she'd never met.

It's as if she's completely forgotten what happened with Freeman. Freeman was Seth's older brother who'd left the Amish ten years earlier to marry an *Englisch* nurse, Kristine, who'd tended to him when he was in the hospital after injuring his back during a barn raising. What made the situation doubly painful was that Kristine initially insisted she wanted to join the Amish and had even quit her job in order to work and live in Willow Creek and learn *Deitsch*. But in the end, she'd decided she couldn't leave her career and lifestyle behind, so Freeman had "gone *Englisch*."

By that time, Seth and Freeman's father—Martha's son—had already died, but their mother was devastated by Freeman's decision. She passed away less than two years later from what the doctor called congestive heart failure, which Seth translated to mean a broken heart. On some level, he blamed his brother's leaving for his mother's death. So, in light of the devastating influence an *Englisch* woman had had on their family, Seth was perplexed that Martha was eager to become involved with another one. But when he voiced his concern, she reminded him what the Bible said about loving one's neighbors. Since he couldn't argue with that, Seth kept his mouth shut, but it troubled him that Martha had wandered off to the little house next door. Her vision was too poor for her to navigate the bumpy yard, even if she did use a cane.

"*Kumme*, Timothy and Tanner. Let's go next door to see if *Groossmammi* is there. On your feet, not on your bellies."

The four-year-old twins were as imaginative as they were energetic, and they reveled in pretending to be various animals. Today they were acting like snakes, and they'd spent the afternoon trying to slither on their stomachs on the banks by the creek.

"Your boots are too dirty to go indoors, so you may play in the front yard. Stay where I can see you," Seth instructed after they crossed their yard to the only house located within half a mile of them. He bounded up the porch stairs, pulled the door open and, before his eyes adjusted to the light, questioned the figure in the kitchen, *"Groossmammi?"*

But it was a young woman who turned from the stove with a teakettle in her hand. Her long dark hair was drawn up in a ponytail, accentuating the sharp angles of her face. Seth knew the *Englisch* considered thinness attractive, but this young woman was so spindly she appeared fragile. Dark eyebrows framed her big, upturned green eyes and her lips were parted as if she were about to speak, but she didn't say a word.

"I'm sorry if I scared you," he said, feeling self-conscious for entering her home uninvited. "My name is Seth Helmuth and I wondered if my *groossmammi*—my grandmother—is here?"

Before the woman had a chance to answer, Martha stepped into the kitchen. "Ah, Seth, there you are. This is Patience Kauffman's *dochder*, Trina Smith."

When Trina held out her hand, Seth reluctantly took it; shaking hands was an *Englisch* practice, not an Amish one. Her fingers were slender and icy but her grip was firm.

"Hello," she said. Closer up, she appeared more mature and taller than she'd seemed at first glance, and her voice had a melodic quality when she gestured toward the kettle, explaining, "Mrs. Helmuth and I were about to have tea."

"Mrs. Helmuth?" Seth repeated with a chuckle because he wasn't used to hearing his grandmother referred to by that title. The Amish didn't use Mr. or Mrs. to address each other; they simply used first names.

"Dear, you can call me Martha," his grandmother said to Trina before giving Seth the eye. No matter that she could hardly see or that he was twenty-eight-years-old, when Martha gave Seth a certain look, he knew he had better watch his step. She told him, "Trina found a mouse in that cupboard over there. I'd like you to take a look."

Seth obediently crossed the room. In his peripheral vision he saw Trina inch even farther away from the cupboard than she already was. Did she think the mouse was going to fly out and nip her nose? He tugged the door open.

"It's empty, but there's a crack in the wood. Since you saw the mouse in daytime, it was probably really hungry and searching for something to eat," he said. Anticipating Martha's request and eager to get out of the house, he added, "I've got a spare trap. I'll go get it. *Groossmammi*, will you watch the *buwe* in the yard until I get back?"

"I'll keep an eye on them, for what good that will do," Martha joked. "You know what my vision is like. When we're inside or they're close by, it's not difficult watching the *buwe*, but when they're running around outdoors..."

"I'll go watch them if you'll stay here and listen for the teakettle," Trina offered, following Seth to the door. "Just give me a call when it whistles."

Seth hesitated to leave his sons in Trina's charge, but since he'd only be gone for a few minutes, he said in *Englisch* to the boys, "Timothy, Tanner, this is, er, this is Miss Smith.

She's going to stay with you while I go get something from our house."

"Miss Smith?" she repeated, pointedly imitating the tone Seth had taken when she referred to Martha as Mrs. Helmuth. "My name is Trina. It starts with the letter T, just like Timothy and Tanner."

The boys raced to her side. "Do you want to see something?" they asked in *Englisch*.

Seth hurried home, grabbed the trap, a jar of peanut butter and a spoon, and then raced back to Trina's house. As he crossed the yard, he spotted the boys and Trina taking turns jumping over a partially frozen mud puddle. Recently the deacon's sons had returned from a family trip to a popular Amish vacation destination in Pinecraft, Florida, and they'd filled Timothy's and Tanner's heads with visions of alligators. Ever since then, the boys pretended puddles were swamps where the toothy creatures hid. They'd created a game in which they had to leap over these so-called swamps without falling in and being bitten. So far, they'd been successful, and it looked as if Trina was holding her own, too. Satisfied they'd all be fine, Seth went inside.

"The tea will be ready soon. Have a cup with us," Martha coaxed him as he smeared peanut butter on the trap. "Trina is a lovely *maedel*. She's a preschool teacher, you know."

"*Jah*, I know," Seth replied. "You've told me almost every day since the attorney told you, *Groossmammi*."

"You ought to consider hiring her to watch the *buwe*, then. She'd be perfect."

Seth glanced out the window. He had to admit, he would have expected someone as thin as Trina to be lethargic but she was matching Timothy and Tanner's energy levels.

"*Neh*, I don't think that would be right. She's *Englisch*."

Martha snickered. "What difference does that make? She seems to know plenty of *Deitsch* words and the *buwe* are almost fluent in *Englisch*. Besides, they'll formally learn *Englisch* as soon as they enter school. This will help them along."

"It's not that," Seth hedged. Even if he wasn't already wary of *Englisch* women because of Freeman's wife, he would have been reluctant to hire one to watch the boys. Seth owned a leather shop in town and he'd seen how *Englisch* customers behaved. In his opinion, the parents were too permissive with their children, allowing them to do and say whatever they wanted.

"Then what is it? Being *Englisch* isn't contagious, you know!"

Martha was so shrewd about his bias that Seth had to try a different approach. "You told me the attorney said she only has to stay here for two months. After that, she'll move on."

"Which is exactly why you should hire her." Martha was really digging her heels in about this. "It's only a little over two months until school lets out and then there will be three or four *meed* vying for the opportunity to earn money taking care of the *buwe*."

"That's right. It's only a couple more months. We can manage until then," Seth insisted. He supposed if worse came to worst and Martha really couldn't handle the boys at home, he could take them to work with him.

"The sooner you get someone to watch the *kinner,* the sooner you'll have an opportunity to visit the matchmaker and begin courting. You won't have to stay home every night in order to give me a break from minding the *buwe*."

Clearly Martha was appealing to Seth's expressed desire to remarry. It had been four years since Eleanor died in childbirth and he was ready to consider courting again.

"I've waited this long. A couple more months

isn't going to make a big difference," Seth replied, but his resolve was wavering.

Martha pointed to the window. "Listen to how much fun they're having out there."

Seth glanced out at them. Just then Trina attempted to hurdle the puddle, but Timothy stepped into her path. Trying to avoid him, she veered and lost her footing upon landing. She fell backward, splintering the puddle's thin layer of ice and landing on Tanner, who hadn't given her enough time to clear it before he jumped over it, too. Seth charged out of the house and down the steps. By then the boys had untangled their legs and arms from Trina's and they were pulling on her hands. Instead of helping her up they were stretching her forward and she struggled to rise.

"Stop that!" he yelled as he noticed Trina's leg was bent awkwardly beneath her. The boys immediately released Trina's hands and she dropped backward into the puddle again.

Thudding onto her backside in the mud a second time, Trina got the wind knocked out of her. Before she had a chance to catch her breath or unfold her leg, Seth slid one arm under her knees, wrapped the other around her waist and swooped her up. As he carried her to the porch, Trina's cheek brushed against his woolen overcoat and she closed her eyes. Never had she felt so cared for by a man and she was overwhelmed by his chivalrous gesture.

"Are you alright?" he asked after gingerly placing her on the porch steps. He leaned forward and looked into her eyes. His own eyes were gunmetal gray, a few shades paler than his sons' baby blues but just as big and round. They'd also inherited Seth's curly blond locks, although his hair was more waves than curls. *Wholesome* was the clichéd word people used to describe anyone who lived in the countryside, but in Seth's case, Trina found the adjective to be accurate. Not merely because of his looks, but because of the honest quality of his concern.

"I'm fine, just a little wet," she replied, embarrassed. She could feel her skirt clinging to her skin.

"I'm sorry," Timothy said mournfully. "I shouldn't have stepped in front of you."

"And I shouldn't have stepped in back of you," Tanner chimed in.

The boys looked so pitifully sad Trina forgot about her own discomposure. "It's nobody's fault but my own. I'm such a klutz," she said, rolling her eyes. When the boys didn't smile, she assured them, "I didn't break any bones.

My skirt got a little dirty, but I'll wash it and it will be as good as new."

Seth looked dubious. "It will get clean, but I doubt it will be as *gut* as new. Abe's house doesn't have an *Englisch* washing machine, you know."

Now Trina couldn't tell if he was speaking matter-of-factly or tongue in cheek. "I'm familiar with Amish wringers," she replied. She was familiar with them in the sense that her mother had described how they worked—Trina hadn't actually used one herself.

"Even so—" Seth started to say, but he was interrupted by a muted cry from inside the house.

"Fire! Help! Help!" It was Martha.

"*Buwe,* stay here!" Seth commanded. He vaulted past Trina and was up the stairs in two strides.

Chasing close behind, Trina peered through the smoky room to see Martha doubled over, coughing, as something burned atop the stove. Seth clicked off the burner, grabbed the flaming item by an edge and tossed it into the sink. Then he turned the faucet on full force.

While he was dousing the flame, Trina led Martha out of the house.

"*Groossmammi*, are you okay?" Tanner asked.

The crease between his eyebrows made him appear like a wizened old man.

Martha nodded but she was still coughing and couldn't answer. Trina and the boys eased her into a sitting position on the stairs and then Trina darted back into the house to fetch a glass of water.

Seth moved away from the sink. "Looks like my *groossmammi* started a towel on fire, but I don't see any other damage. Is she alright?"

"Yes, I think so. She just needs to catch her breath." Trina filled the glass and they both stepped outside, leaving the door open behind them.

By then, Martha was no longer gasping. "I spilled water on the stovetop when I was pouring tea, so I tried to dab it up with the towel," she explained. "I was certain I had turned off the burner first."

"*Neh,* you had turned it *up*," Seth said.

"Ach! Well, that explains how the tea towel caught fire." Martha's eyes were watering and Trina didn't know if she was crying or recovering from the sting of the smoky air. Suddenly Martha seemed tiny and frail as she prayed aloud, "*Denki,* Lord, for keeping us safe."

"It's cold out here and you're trembling," Trina noticed. "Please come back inside and we'll have that tea now."

"Alright," Martha agreed. "Seth, *kumme* get the woodstove started, please."

Trina took Martha by the arm and assisted her up the stairs and into the parlor. She expected the others to come in, too, but when she returned to the kitchen to retrieve the tea, she heard Seth on the porch warning the boys not to leave the front yard or go near the puddle.

"They're probably cold, too. They should come in," she said from the doorway.

"*Neh*, their boots are muddy." Seth waved his hand. "They're fine outside. Here in Willow Creek, we believe fresh air is *gut* for *kinner*."

Once again Trina wasn't sure what he meant by his remark. She replied, "We believe fresh air is good for children in Philadelphia, too."

"*Jah*, but there's less of it in Philadelphia than there is here, so our *kinner* can stay outside longer." Seth grinned widely at her before he began filling his arms with logs from the woodpile stacked next to the porch stairs, and since she didn't disagree, Trina chuckled, too.

As she and Martha were sipping tea and Seth was lighting the fire, the older woman said, "Imagine what would have happened if you weren't here!"

Seth stood up from where he'd been kneeling in front of the woodstove and brushed his hands against his pants. His grandmother had a valid point and he knew she was waiting for him to acknowledge defeat. "Okay, okay, you win," he said to Martha.

Trina glanced at Martha and then at him, curious.

"I, uh, well, we wanted to ask if you'd be available to watch the *buwe* while you're in Willow Creek," he stuttered. "As a job, I mean. You'd be paid."

"You could watch them at our house, so I could help and we'd get to know each other better," Martha added, beaming again.

Trina hesitated. Although the will stipulated she had to live in Willow Creek, she hadn't intended to become very involved with the Amish—or the *Englisch*, for that matter— during her residence. She'd planned to mostly keep to herself. But the boys were well behaved and fun, and after today's incident she hated to think of Martha trying to manage them on her own. Still, she had her misgivings about Seth. He wasn't as strict as she imagined an Amish father might be, based on her mother's depiction of Abe, yet there was something about his attitude toward her that gave her pause. She couldn't discern whether his comments were meant to be comical or condescending. But Martha had been so helpful to Trina's mother that it would almost be like honoring her mother's memory to show Timothy and Tanner the same kind of care. And she did need the money...

"I'm only going to be here for a couple of months," she warned. As soon as her two months were up and she sold the house, she was moving back to the city.

Seth replied, "That's all the time we'll need your help. After school lets out in late May, we'll hire one of the graduating *meed* to help. But right now, no one else is available to watch them."

"Okay, it's a deal," Trina said, but this time she didn't hold her hand out to shake on it. She was already catching on to Willow Creek's Amish traditions.

Martha leaned on Seth's arm, slowly shambling across the barren ground to their house while the boys galloped ahead. If he didn't know better, he'd have suspected his grandmother deliberately started the fire to scare him into asking Trina to mind the boys.

"Why are you moping?" Martha asked him.

"I'm not moping. I'm thinking."

"When you're thinking with a frown on your face, I call that moping."

Seth laughed. "I hope I made the right decision by asking Trina to watch after the *buwe*."

"Pah!" Martha sputtered dismissively. "It's not as if you've asked her to marry you, Seth. If things don't work out, you can tell her as much. But I think they will. If she's anything like her lovely *mamm* was as a *maedel*, you won't find a better woman to care for the *kinner*."

Seth bit his tongue so he wouldn't ask the obvious question: if Trina's *mamm* was so lovely, why did she go *Englisch*? Nor did he say that the best woman to care for the *kinner* was their *mamm*.

Eleanor's pregnancy had been an easy one, especially considering she was pregnant with twins, so when she'd passed away during childbirth, it had come as a shock to Seth. Eleanor, however, had seemed to have a sense of foreboding about her delivery.

Once, shortly before the boys were born, she'd whispered to Seth as they cuddled on the sofa, "If anything happens to me, please choose a wife who will take *gut* care of the *bobblin*."

"If anything happens to you, I'm going to look for a wife who doesn't burn the meatloaf. Or chide me when I track mud across the kitchen floor. Or say *lecherich* things," Seth joked, trying to make light of her sentiment.

Usually she played along with Seth's teasing, but this time Eleanor had scolded, "Seth, I'm serious." She'd rubbed her rotund stomach counterclockwise, repeating, "Marry someone who will take *gut* care of the *kinner*."

Although Seth knew it was irrational, he often wondered if he had taken Eleanor's sentiment seriously, could he have alerted the midwife to her concern and somehow prevented her death? He felt guilty for not paying closer attention to what Eleanor had said, especially since she'd ordinarily been such a calm and practical woman.

In fact, it was her practicality that had made Seth decide to court and marry her. The pair had been friends since they were children and Eleanor was sensible, forthright and humble. While the love they shared was more comfortable than ardent, it had been rich and deep. No, Seth couldn't claim he and Eleanor had ever "fallen in love," like Freeman had with Kristine, but look at all the hurt that kind of love had caused his family. Passionate emotional attachment wasn't important to Seth; compatibility, commitment and common sense were. He and Eleanor had found those qualities in each other and their marriage had been a strong and happy one.

With Martha caring for the boys after Eleanor's death, Seth felt little need to remarry at all, which was why he hadn't courted anyone in the over four years since Timothy and Tanner were born. But now, given his *groossmammi*'s declining vision, he understood the wisdom in Eleanor's request. The boys needed someone to care for them. Not just a teenage *maedel* and certainly not just an *Englischer* for a few months. They needed a permanent mother figure.

As Martha tottered along beside him, Seth figured maybe his grandmother was right; now that Trina would be watching the boys he'd have more time to work on finding a wife. Meanwhile, he hoped Trina's *Englisch* ways wouldn't unduly influence his sons. Seth was going to have to keep a close eye on her.

The prospect should have troubled him more than it did. Maybe he'd let his guard down because Martha had taken an instant liking to Trina, but Seth was oddly amused by the skinny woman with mischievous eyes and a musical voice, and he rather enjoyed trying to get a rise out of her. How much influence could she have on his family in two months anyway?

Chapter Two

After Seth and Martha left, Trina washed the cups and began unpacking her suitcase. It didn't take long. By the time she moved out of her apartment, she'd either sold or given away nearly all of her belongings and she only had a few outfits that were suitable to wear in Amish country. It wouldn't be appropriate to dress like the Amish, but out of respect for the people she was living among she decided she'd wear dresses or skirts instead of slacks or jeans. Unfortunately, she only owned one dress and three skirts—one of which was now very dirty.

The only nonclothing items she'd brought were a framed photograph and her cell phone and solar battery charger. The photo was of her and her mother and it had been taken on a beach when they went to Cape Cod for a rare week of vacation the summer before Patience got sick. Trina had other photos saved digitally, but it was this printed one she cherished the most. In it, they were both smiling, healthy and tan, and their cheeks touched as they leaned together in a sideways embrace. One rainy afternoon as Trina and her mother strolled through the art galleries, admiring the paintings and sculptures they couldn't afford, they'd come across an ornate picture frame. Handmade from small pieces of aqua, green and blue sea glass the artist found on the bayside, the frame reminded Trina of the ocean itself. That Christmas, Trina's mother presented her with the frame as a gift. Trina never knew how she managed to pay for it or sneak away to buy it, but combined with the photo it held, it was Trina's one and only prized possession.

She considered keeping the photo on the dresser in her room, so it could be the first thing she saw when she awoke, but then she decided she wanted to put it in a more visible area, somewhere she could see it all the time and draw strength from the memory. She carried it into the parlor and placed it prominently on the end table next to the sofa.

Then she considered where to store her cell phone. It wasn't as if she'd be receiving any calls. Trina had moved to a new suburb shortly before her mother was diagnosed with cancer. She was acquainted with other teachers there but she hadn't begun to make friends. And the church she attended was so big no one there was likely to notice her absence. Yet, knowing she'd probably need to be in touch with a realtor as well as the estate attorney her grandfather hired, Trina had purchased a solar panel charger to power her phone. She decided to set it up on the windowsill in Abe's old bedroom, where it would get plenty of sunshine but be out of her way.

Exhausted from cleaning her apartment, packing up and traveling, Trina changed into her nightgown. She slipped beneath the quilt, which smelled of fresh winter air—Martha must have hung it on the clothesline—and shut her eyes, thinking of how protected she felt when Seth carried her to the porch. Within minutes she drifted into a deep slumber for the first time in over a year.

She woke to a banging on the door. Disoriented, she blinked several times at her surroundings. It was morning. She was in Willow Creek. The fire must have died out because the floor made her feet ache with cold. She wrapped the quilt around her shoulders and shuffled to the door. Peeking out the window, she saw Seth pacing back and forth. *Oh no!*

I was supposed to be at his house by seven forty-five so he could review the rules for the children with me.

"It's eight o'clock," Seth said in greeting. "Look at you, you're not even dressed yet."

Trina pulled her quilt tighter around her shoulders. She understood the Amish didn't place a high value on physical appearance, except for tidiness and modesty. She could only imagine how rumpled she appeared. "I'm so sorry. I must have overslept."

"I thought you *Englischers* relied on alarm clocks."

Rankled, she cracked, "I figured the Amish rooster would wake me."

Something resembling a grin crinkled the skin around Seth's eyes, but he didn't allow it to move to his lips. "Just *kumme* to my house as soon as you can."

She pulled on her clothes, brushed her hair into a ponytail and quickly scrubbed her teeth before running across the yard. When she arrived, she apologized again. "I really am sorry I'm late. I didn't mean to oversleep."

Seth seemed less cantankerous now. "It's alright. Fresh air can tucker a person out." There it was again; the kind of comment that made her wonder if he was joking or not.

"*Guder mariye*, Trina," Martha said as she

entered the room, her hands extended in front of her so as not to bump into anything. It seemed she only used her cane outdoors. Timothy and Tanner scooted around their grandmother, calling out their greetings, as well. Their curls bounced as they hopped up and down, unable to contain their excitement.

"Guder mariye," Trina replied to the three of them.

"We're going to show you the creek today," Tanner announced.

"Neh, I don't want you by the creek," Seth contradicted. "It's too dangerous. The current is too strong."

The boys looked crestfallen but they didn't argue. Didn't they tell Trina they'd been to the creek just yesterday? It hadn't rained, so the water couldn't be any deeper. Then she realized Seth must not trust her with the children yet. She understood. In time, he'd change his mind.

"I'm sure we'll do something else that's just as interesting," Trina said.

"Jah, so will you and I," Martha chimed in. "When they take a nap, you can look through my fabric to choose what you want to make a new skirt since yours became stained yesterday."

Trina appreciated the offer, but she had no

idea how to make a skirt. "Oh, that's alright. The stain will come out. My skirt is still wearable."

"With the way you'll be running after the *buwe,* it won't hurt to have an extra one," Martha said. "If it's the material you're worried about, don't be concerned. I have an assortment of colors. Blue, green, even burgundy. I haven't been able to see well enough to sew for ages. It will be *gut* to know the fabric isn't going to waste."

"I don't think it's the color of the fabric she's worried about, *Groossmammi,*" Seth quietly pointed out. "The *Englisch* don't sew like we do."

Trina bristled. Why did Seth constantly call attention to how different the *Englisch* were from the Amish? "Don't be *lecherich.* Plenty of *Englischers* sew their own clothes." She used a couple of *Deitsch* words to emphasize she wasn't completely unaware of Amish culture.

"And you're one of them?" Seth pressed.

Trina felt her cheeks burning. Her mother had tried to teach her to sew, but Trina never had the inclination. "Yes, I can sew my own clothes. I can hem them, anyway."

Seth snorted. "It's not the same thing."

"Just how much do you know about sewing

clothes?" Martha chastised him. "As fine as your leather stitching is, I have yet to see you make your own britches, my dear *bu*."

Trina's gratitude for the woman surged. It was obvious Seth wouldn't contend with Martha. He set his hat on his head and buttoned his wool coat.

"The *buwe*'s chore for the day is to rid the front yard of sticks," he instructed Trina. "And they must lie down for an hour in the afternoon, whether they sleep or not."

"Don't worry," Martha said, answering for Trina. "I'll fill Trina in on everything she needs to know. Now, since you were so worried about being late, you'd better skedaddle."

After the door closed behind Seth, Trina released her breath. In her experience as a teacher, the parents were often more difficult to manage than the preschoolers were. *I should tell Seth that's* one *way the* Englisch *and the Amish are alike,* she thought, chuckling to herself.

Because Seth was in a hurry, he'd forgotten to put on his gloves so he blew on his fingers as he walked to town. He could have taken the buggy, but that would have meant leaving his shop several times a day to make sure the horse was watered, fed and dry—and it looked like rain. Or snow. It was difficult to tell at this time of year.

Besides, he liked the walk and the shop was only about a mile and a half away. He used the time to mentally prepare for work and ask the Lord to guide him in his interactions with the customers, especially the *Englisch* ones. When Seth moved from Ohio to Willow Creek, all the stores on Main Street were taken. He'd made it his goal to one day open a shop there, because that's where most of the *Englisch* customers and tourists came through town. While he had a healthy business selling harnesses and other horse leatherworks to the Amish, the *Englisch* had little need for such items. Instead, they wanted custom-designed purses, belts and wallets, and they wanted them at their convenience.

Since the workshop at his home was slightly off the beaten path, Seth had recognized that, in order to increase business, he had to meet his customers' needs—or their preferences—and he watched and waited for one of the Amish business owners to relinquish their prime real estate on Main Street. When one of the bigger spaces recently opened up, Seth jumped at the chance to lease it. It was a stretch for him financially, but the space was so big it allowed him to have a workshop in the back in addition to the storefront where he could display and sell his wares. He figured in time the sales would be worth the initial investment.

Now that I'm paying Trina to watch the buwe, *I'll have an added expense I hadn't counted on until school lets out,* he thought.

As he contemplated his sons' care, Seth asked the Lord to watch over Trina as she cared for the boys. Once again he second-guessed his decision to hire her. Martha seemed to think highly of Trina, but then, his grandmother had an unusual gift for making people feel welcome and needed—that's how Seth felt when he moved in with the boys, who were only newborns at the time. What would he have done without Martha's help? He supposed the least he could do now was make more of an effort to show a modicum of hospitality toward Trina, since Martha had shown an abundance toward him.

He was so lost in thought that when he arrived at his shop, he was startled to find three *Englisch* women standing on the doorstep, peeking through the window into the store. In his experience, the *Englisch* customers tended to be more impatient than the Amish. It seemed to him *Englischers* were often in a rush and they expected others to be in a rush, too, whereas Seth felt if he couldn't do a job both quickly and well, he'd rather do it well than quickly.

"We were afraid you were closed for the day!" one of them said.

"*Neh*, just for the first ten minutes," Seth replied with a grin as he keyed into the shop. He found humor often kept him from becoming too stressed and his customers appreciated it, too. Especially the *Englisch* ones, who often seemed taken aback initially, as if they were under the impression the Amish were humorless dullards. But they usually ended up smiling back.

Sure enough, the women giggled as Seth held the door open for them. Soon after, a few more customers trickled in. Seth noticed one of them discreetly lifting a cell phone and he knew he was being photographed. He had half a mind to post a sign forbidding cell phones and cameras in the store, but he decided if people weren't going to voluntarily respect his beliefs and privacy, it was useless to try to *make* them do so.

By the end of the day he was relieved to walk home and when he went through the door, the boys bounded into the kitchen to greet him as they usually did.

"Guess what, *Daed*," Tanner said. "Trina taught us an *Englisch* song."

"And we had lots and lots of vegetation for dinner," Timothy claimed.

"You mean vegetables," Seth corrected him.

"*Neh*, it was vegetation."

Just then Trina entered the room and said above the boys' heads, "*Hungerich* bucks need a lot of vegetation to stay strong."

Ah, so that was it. Seth had to smile. He and Martha had a difficult time getting the boys to eat any vegetables except potatoes and corn. If Trina had been able to get the boys to eat more greens by appealing to their interest in animals, that was terrific. But he drew the line at teaching them *Englisch* songs.

"*Buwe,* please go into the other room while I talk to Trina," he said. After they scampered away, he asked Trina how her day went.

"It was *gut*," she said. He noticed she was using *Deitsch* words more frequently already. "The *buwe* picked up the sticks in the front yard and half the sticks on the west side of the house, too. They sure have a lot of energy."

Seth nodded before getting to the point. "They said you taught them an *Englisch* song. May I hear it?"

He saw a look of confusion pass over Trina's face before her cheeks broke into a blush. He regretted embarrassing her, but he had to be sure the boys weren't being taught songs about superheroes or other ideas that were contrary to Amish beliefs.

"It's more like a poem than a song. At least it was the way I presented it," she said and her usually mellifluous voice was marked with defiance.

"All the same, I'd like to hear it."

Trina exhaled audibly and then began, "One, two, buckle my shoe…" She continued reciting the verse until she got to the number ten, at which point she said, "That's as high as we went. I was trying to teach them how to count while they were doing yard work."

"I see," Seth said. He'd been taught that same verse as a child and he felt as foolish as he'd obviously made Trina feel. Still, he wasn't sorry he asked her to tell him how the song went. "We didn't have time this morning to discuss what kinds of activities are appropriate for Amish *kinner*, so I just wanted to be sure—"

"There you are, Seth," Martha interrupted from the doorway. "It smells like supper is about ready, isn't it, Trina?"

Trina peeked inside the oven. "*Jah,* it's bubbling," she confirmed, removing the pan from the rack and setting the chicken-and-cheese casserole on a hot pad on the table. "You should let it cool a bit before you eat it. And don't forget the asparagus. It's steaming on the back burner."

"I thought you were going to stay for supper. You know we made plenty," Martha said.

So much for demonstrating hospitality; Seth knew he was the reason Trina changed her mind about supping with them. "*Jah*, you should stay," he echoed.

"*Denki*, but I need to be on my way. I'll arrive a few minutes early tomorrow, Seth, so we'll have plenty of time to review your list of restrictions about the *kinner* with me."

"There's no *list*," he mumbled feebly, but Trina didn't seem to hear as she zipped her jacket. Unfortunately, Martha was listening intently, and from the look on her face, Seth was going to get an earful about his attitude tonight after the boys were in bed.

Completely humiliated, Trina slinked home. After spending most of the morning and afternoon outside with the boys, her appetite was raging in a way she hadn't experienced since before her mother took ill. But there'd been no way she was going to sit down at a table with that smug, controlling Seth Helmuth. She respected that Amish people abided by their church's *Ordnung*, and without knowing what it said herself, it was possible she might have accidentally violated one of its precepts. But she'd felt like a criminal when Seth demanded she recite the song like that. She hoped he felt utterly ridiculous when he heard how it went!

In the kitchen, she removed her jacket and hung it on the peg beside the door. Almost immediately she took it back down and put it on again. It was freezing in there. Now she was cold as well as hungry. How was she going to go grocery shopping? The stores within walking distance closed by the time Seth returned home and she didn't have a car. What was she going to subsist on? Water and Willow Creek's superior fresh air?

She went into the parlor and lit a fire in the woodstove. Then she looked around for her handbag, which contained half a packet of crackers with peanut butter she'd bought at the train station. When she found it, she gobbled a cracker and then brought the rest into the kitchen where she put the kettle on to fix a cup of the tea Martha had left for her. Once the water came to a boil, Trina filled a mug, put the crackers on a plate and sat down next to the woodstove.

Even with her jacket on and the warm cup in her hands, she was shivering, so she retrieved the quilt from her bed and wrapped herself in it before returning to her chair. The silence was punctuated only by the ticking clock and Trina understood why her mother had felt like time stood still in Willow Creek. Trina had only been there two days and it already seemed like a lifetime. It was enough to make her want to pack her bags right then.

Of course, Trina's mother had had a far more significant reason to leave Willow Creek behind: Abe Kauffman. But as miserable as her mother's life with Abe had been, she'd rarely spoken against him in detail. Patience had only described how, after her own mother died, her father changed.

"Mind you, he never lifted a hand against me," she told Trina. "But he wouldn't lift a hand toward me, either. Not to help me, not to embrace me. He hardly spoke a word to me. It was as if I didn't exist—as if I had died when my mother did. All that existed was his bottle of beer. So, in a way, I felt as if he'd died, too. At eight years of age, I felt orphaned."

No wonder her mother had never wanted to return to this house. When Trina was young and used to ask her mother if they could visit Willow Creek, Patience's face would cloud with sadness as she said no, it was better for everyone if they didn't. "We're happy right where we are, aren't we?" she'd ask Trina, and Trina always answered yes because it was true. As long as they were together, they were happy. Trina sniffed as she realized her mother would never be with her again. Did that mean Trina would never be happy again, either? She knew she couldn't allow herself to dwell on such thoughts or she'd never make it through her time in Willow Creek, so she prayed the Lord would give her peace and then she went to draw a bath.

But before she reached the washroom, there was a knock at the door. In the kitchen, Trina peered through the door's glass pane to see Seth holding a plate wrapped in tin foil in one hand and Martha's basket from yesterday in the other.

"Yes?" she said coldly after opening the door.

"My *groossmammi* sent these for you," he replied, lifting the items in her direction.

Since they were from Martha, Trina couldn't refuse them. "Please tell her I said *denki*." She reached for the plate but Seth held on to the basket, stepping into the kitchen uninvited.

"How's the mouse situation?" he asked. "Did the trap do the trick?"

"I don't know. I haven't checked."

He set the basket on the table, crossed the room and pried the cupboard open. To Trina's relief, he announced, "*Neh*, nothing yet." Then he closed the cupboard and rubbed his arms.

"Seems a little cold in here. I can show you how to get a *gut* fire roaring if you'd like."

Trina didn't know why he was suddenly being so congenial, but she wished he'd leave. Not just because she was still miffed, but because the aroma of the meal he brought was making her feel even more famished and she could hardly wait to eat. "Actually, I'm rather warm," she said, tossing her ponytail.

"I imagine you are," Seth replied, his lips twitching. "Wearing a quilt has that effect on people."

Trina rolled her eyes and shrugged the quilt from her shoulders. She folded it into a misshapen square, which she held in front of her stomach to muffle the growling sound it was making. "I suppose I could add another log to the fire."

"I'll grab a couple more from outside, since the bin in the parlor is probably low," Seth volunteered and exited the house before Trina could object.

As soon as he left, Trina lifted an edge of the tinfoil from the plate and dug into the casserole with a fork. When Seth returned, her mouth was full, but she mumbled, "*Denki* for bringing those in, but I've gone camping before, so I'm capable of stoking the fire myself."

"Is that what you think being Amish means? It's like going camping?"

Why was he suddenly defensive again? "No, that's what I think *lighting a fire* is like," Trina clarified after swallowing. "If you've built one outside, you can build one inside."

"Actually, that's not necessarily true. *Kumme*, let me show you."

She reluctantly put her supper down and went into the parlor with him.

"Ah," he said when he opened the door to the woodstove. "Look at this."

Trina crouched down beside him. She watched his hands gesturing as he spoke, oddly aware those were the same strong hands that had lifted her the day before.

"You've done alright with the kindling, but you've piled the logs too tightly together," he explained, not unkindly. "There needs to be a little room between them for the oxygen to get through. Otherwise, the logs won't take and the flame will burn out like it has now. It's better if you stack them like this."

As she listened to him, it occurred to Trina he would make a good teacher. She glanced sideways at his face, noticing the reddish undertone to his short beard. She wondered if it would feel like his wool coat had felt against her cheek. Suddenly her skin burned and she knew she couldn't attribute its warmth to the fire now crackling in the stove.

"Denki," she said, standing up.

Seth rose, too, saying, "I want to apologize if I embarrassed you when I asked you to tell me the song you taught the *buwe.*"

If Trina's face hadn't felt hot before, it would have now under Seth's earnest gaze. "It's alright," she conceded, and suddenly, it was.

She realized if a virtual stranger—especially one who had traditions that were different from her own—came to watch her children, she'd give them guidelines about what the kids could and couldn't do. In fact, when she used to babysit as a teenager, parents always told her what the house rules were. It wasn't personal, she'd just taken it that way because of Seth's comments about her being *Englisch.* But maybe she was the one who was being defensive because he was Amish, instead of vice versa. Or maybe it was a little of both.

"I respect the way you're raising your *kinner* and I want to instruct the *buwe* according to your guidelines," she said. "Do you have a few minutes to talk about that now?"

"Jah." Seth grinned, and his jawline visibly softened as he sank into the sofa.

First, Trina hoped she put Seth's mind at ease by telling him she shared his strong

Christian faith. Then they briefly discussed his expectations of the boys as well as their interests and the activities they were forbidden to do. Nothing Seth mentioned seemed unduly prohibitive or out of the ordinary to Trina, but she was glad they'd had the discussion anyway.

"I'll see you tomorrow morning, then?" Seth confirmed as he was leaving.

Did Trina catch a note of uncertainty in his voice? "*Jah*, I'll be there bright and early at seven forty-five," she assured him.

"Then I'll be sure to set the rooster for six forty-five," he said over his shoulder before closing the door, and Trina laughed in spite of herself.

Her supper had cooled but she didn't care. The casserole was so delicious she couldn't believe she'd made it herself—well, with advice from Martha. Trina never had much interest in cooking, aside from a few traditional Amish desserts her mother taught her to make. Usually by the time she returned home from work she was so hungry and worn out she would just to throw a meal into the microwave.

She was pleased to see the basket contained eggs, milk and half a loaf of bread. Martha was as thoughtful and generous as Trina's mother had said she was. Her tummy full, Trina washed the dishes and before she got ready for bed, she retrieved her cell phone and set its alarm. She didn't want to be late again, especially now that she and Seth were on better terms with each other.

Once he'd cleared the air with Trina, Seth felt more comfortable having her mind the boys, who relished their time with her. Each evening when he came to the door, they regaled him with anecdotes about the adventures they'd had with her during the day. And although his grandmother had always been lively, she seemed even sprightlier now. Seth couldn't tell whether that was because Trina had taken over the boy's care, or because Martha enjoyed having the company of another woman, but he was pleased the arrangement was off to a good start.

On Saturday he woke to the racket of raindrops pummeling the rooftop and he eased out of bed. After milking the cow, he collected eggs from the henhouse. Usually this was Tanner and Timothy's responsibility, but it was raining too hard to allow them to go outside.

When Seth returned to the house, Tanner was standing in the kitchen, knuckling his eyes sleepily. "*Daed*, is it time for Trina to *kumme* yet?"

"She doesn't *kumme* until you and your

brother have changed into your clothes, eaten your breakfast and brushed your teeth. I already collected the *oier* because it's raining and I don't want you to go outside today unless it stops."

"We're teaching Trina how to collect *oier*, too, but she's afraid to put her hand in the coop. She thinks the *hinkel* will peck her. *Groossmammi* told us it isn't kind to laugh at her so we never do," Tanner reported solemnly. Then he corrected himself, admitting, "We did laugh the first time, *Daed*. But we never do anymore. Not even when she's scared and she jumps like this."

Tanner's imitation of Trina's jitters reminded Seth of how she'd flinched when he opened the cupboard to check for the mouse, and he suppressed a chuckle. "*Groossmammi* is right. It isn't kind to laugh at Trina. Most *Englischers* buy their eggs in a store, but in time she'll learn how to collect *oier* from the henhouse. Now go wake your brother."

Tanner obediently thumped back upstairs. Meanwhile, Martha shuffled into the room. Anticipating her question, Seth said, "*Guder mariye, Groossmammi*. I haven't made *kaffi* yet but I'll get it started as soon as I put these *oier* in the pot to boil."

"*Denki*, but I can fix breakfast for us." Martha removed a pot from the cupboard. With her back to him, she added, "Don't stand there watching me. I still know my way around a pot of *oier*. I only had an accident the other day because I wasn't used to Abe's stove."

Seth left the room to wash his hands, returning a few minutes later with Timothy and Tanner. After breakfast Martha served coffee while the boys went to brush their teeth.

Seth took a long pull from his mug and then said, "I probably won't be home until around suppertime tonight."

"Why not? You don't keep the shop open past two o'clock on Saturdays during winter."

Even though his grandmother knew he intended to eventually visit a matchmaker in the neighboring Elmsville district, Seth felt embarrassed to remind her about it now. "I, uh, I'm going to see Belinda Imhoff this afternoon."

Martha stopped sipping her coffee. "Ah, I see. Then I guess we'll have to do our shopping at the *Englisch* market tonight instead of the one on Main Street this afternoon."

"If you write out a list for me, I can pick up what you need before I set off to Elmsville. It's chilly enough that the perishables will keep in the buggy until I get home."

"*Neh*, I'd rather go. It will get me out of

the house. Besides, Trina will need to *kumme* shopping, too."

"Trina? With us?" Seth questioned.

"*Jah*. In case you haven't noticed, she doesn't have a car and it wouldn't do her any *gut* to walk to the market in town, since it's closed by the time you return in the evenings. I don't know how she has any stamina to keep up with the boys. I try to get her to eat more at dinnertime, but she refuses. I think she feels as if she should bring her own dinner, which is *lecherich*."

"*Neh*, I doubt that's it. She's probably just on a diet. You know how the *Englisch* are."

"I know how *people* are. *Englisch* or Amish, they need food in their houses."

Seth pulled on his beard. As grateful as he was for Trina's help, he worried about the boys becoming confused about her role in their lives. This was only a temporary employment situation. If Martha kept treating Trina like one of the family, it could lead to disappointment for Timothy and Tanner once she left.

"I don't think it's a *gut* idea for her to accompany us to the market," he said.

"*Jah*, you're right." Martha gave in so easily it surprised Seth—until she proposed, "She'd probably prefer going to the market alone anyway. So, instead of going to see Belinda Imhoff this afternoon, perhaps you could *kumme* home and teach Trina how to hitch the buggy and handle the horse. That way, she'll be all set to go to the market on her own during the day on Monday. I'll watch the *kinner* while she's gone. If they're napping, it shouldn't be a problem."

Seth shook his head incredulously. "*Neh.* She's not going to use my horse and buggy any more than I'd drive her car."

"*Gut.* Then you'll put off going to Elmsville this afternoon so we can all make it to the market in town before it closes," Martha stated as if it were a done deed.

Although frustrated, Seth knew he couldn't compete with his grandmother's cunning logic. "Alright. She can accompany us to the *Englisch* store in Highland Springs tonight."

His grandmother smiled in his direction. "The *buwe* will be delighted."

On that note, Timothy and Tanner scrambled into the room, dragged a chair to the window and climbed atop it together to watch for Trina.

"There she is," shouted Timothy. They got down and ran to open the door.

"Hurry, Trina. It's raining!" Tanner called, as if she wasn't aware.

"*Guder mariye,*" she sang out, shaking raindrops from her long hair after she hung up her jacket. "What a *wunderbaar* day."

"You're joking now but wait until you've been shut indoors all day," Seth said. "I don't want the *buwe* going outside. Do you hear me, Timothy and Tanner?"

"Jah, Daed," they choroused.

"That's alright. We're going to play a rainy-day animal game inside. It's called Noah's Ark," Trina promised and the boys capered in circles around her. Turning to Seth she added, "If I remember correctly, Bible stories are permitted, *jah*?"

Seth's ears and forehead stung. She was being cheeky, but it didn't feel offensive like the brazen remarks some of his *Englisch* customers made. "Of course Bible stories are allowed, provided they're in German, since that's the language our Bibles are printed in and the language our preachers speak when they're delivering a sermon."

"Naturlich werde ich sprechen Deutsche." In German Trina said of course *she'd* speak in German. Seth had only meant to be facetious. He didn't realize she actually knew the language. Once again, he felt his face flush.

But his ultimate embarrassment came when his grandmother bid him goodbye. *"Mach's gut,* Seth. I hope your meeting with the matchmaker goes well. We'll have supper on the table and you can tell us all about it tonight!"

The youth in Willow Creek usually made a rigorous effort to keep their courtships private, even from their family members. Since Seth had already been married once, he didn't exercise the same level of discretion about courtship when speaking with his grandmother now as he would have when he was younger. Still, he was thoroughly abashed to have her announce his intention of going to a matchmaker in front of Trina. Realizing his humiliation wasn't so much because Trina was *Englisch* as it was because she was a woman, he couldn't get out of the house fast enough.

Chapter Three

Trina felt sorry for Seth. He clearly was embarrassed that Martha had said anything about him going to a matchmaker, especially in front of her. But the boys clamored for Trina's attention and she turned her focus to them.

"How do we play Noah's Ark?" Timothy asked.

"We start by reading Noah's story in the Bible," Trina told them. They sat on the braided rug in front of the woodstove while Trina read to them from the book of Genesis and Martha listened from her spot in the rocking chair. When Trina finished the passage, she instructed the boys to go into the hall and agree on an animal to imitate. When Trina called them into the room, which they were pretending was an ark, they were to enter as a pair, miming their chosen animal. If Trina guessed what they were, they'd go back into the hall and return as a different pair of animals. The boys loved the game and Trina and Martha were entertained by their imitations.

"You have such a way with *kinner*," Martha later complimented her as she and Trina were preparing dinner together.

"Denki." Trina placed the bread Martha had coached her to make on the cutting board.

"You'll make a *wunderbaar mamm* someday soon, too," Martha said. "Is there a special man in your life in Philadelphia? Someone you're…how do the *Englisch* say it? Dating?"

"Jah," Trina responded absentmindedly. The bread hadn't risen as high as she anticipated it would and it seemed tough. "I mean, *jah,* we call it dating. But *neh,* I'm not dating anyone."

Martha clicked her tongue. "Those *Englisch* men can't be too smart to let such a kind, bright and becoming *maedel* like you pass them by."

Trina laughed. "I don't meet that many *Englisch* men. Most of my time is spent at school where there are only two male teachers and both are married. I've dated a couple of men I knew from church, but those relationships didn't last. Besides, I'm not really interested in getting married." She extended the loaf of bread in Martha's direction. "Does this feel hard to you?"

Martha took it from her. "Perhaps. The rainy weather probably affected the yeast."

"Oh, *neh*. I wanted it to turn out!"

"It's alright, dear. The *buwe* won't mind."

It wasn't the boys Trina was worried about; it was Seth. For some reason, she wanted to prove to him she wasn't the microwaving sort of cook he probably took her for. Even if she was.

After they'd eaten dinner, Martha had intended to tell the boys a story while Trina cleaned up in the kitchen, but the older woman had a *koppweh*, a headache.

"It's the light," she explained. "If there's a white glare like there is today, it bothers my eyes. If I turn on a lamp at night, I see halos. If I'm out in the sun, my eyes hurt then, too."

"Would you like an aspirin?" Trina offered.

"I'm afraid we're out. That was one of the items on my grocery list."

"I might have some at my house. Let me run over and get them."

"Can we *kumme*?" the boys pleaded, but Trina reminded them their father said they couldn't go out in the rain, so she dashed home by herself.

She quickly searched her toiletry bag, but

she hadn't any bottles of aspirin in it. There was, however, a pair of sunglasses. Maybe they would help. Trina slipped them into her pocket and bounded back to Seth and Martha's house.

"Oh, that does feel better, dear. *Denki,*" Martha said after she'd put the lenses on over her own glasses.

"*Groossmammi,* you look *voll schpass.*" Of course Tanner would think she looked very funny; he'd probably never seen mirrored lenses before.

"I can see me in your eyes," Timothy declared. He made a funny face in front of Martha and studied his reflection.

"*Buwe,* I'd like you to help me in the kitchen. Tanner, you may sweep while Timothy brings the dirty plates to the sink," Trina instructed. Then she asked Martha if she could get her anything else, but Martha said she was just going to sit there and take a quick catnap.

"*Katze* don't nap sitting up. They curl around like this." Timothy fell to the floor to demonstrate. Chuckling, Trina beckoned him to his feet again.

"*Daed* says we can't have *katze* in the house," Tanner explained as he followed Trina and Timothy. "*Groossmammi*'s 'lergic. That means she sneezes when she touches *katz* fur."

Trina suddenly understood their fascination

with pretending to be animals. "Do you know what makes me sneeze? It starts with the letter S." She emphasized the S sound.

"Snakes?"

"Skunks?"

"*Neh*. Soap!" Trina exclaimed as she scooped a handful of dish soap bubbles over the boys' heads and pretended to sneeze, blowing the bubbles everywhere. Timothy and Tanner whooped and tried to catch them. Despite their exuberance, it was time for their nap, so when they finished cleaning the kitchen, Trina tucked them into their beds and returned to the parlor where Martha was rummaging through a bag of fabric.

"I thought you were going to rest," Trina commented.

"I did. Now let's get you started on making a new skirt."

Martha instructed Trina how to take her measurements and began guiding her through creating a pattern. Trina made so many erasures she figured that even though Martha's vision was impaired the older woman could do a better job of it.

"It's alright. Take your time," Martha said the fourth time Trina botched her penciling. As Trina erased the markings, Martha hummed, but it wasn't a hymn from the *Ausbund*.

"My *mamm* taught me that one," Trina said and sang a few lines. "She usually hummed or sang while she was sewing. Did she learn to do that from you?"

Martha smiled. "More likely, I learned to do that from her. Sometimes when Patience used to *kumme* over, we'd sit here sewing together. If we weren't talking, she was always humming or singing. At the time, my husband, Jacob, thought it was because she was so happy."

Trina stopped erasing. "But you knew that wasn't the reason," she said quietly, knowing the answer.

"*Jah*, I knew it wasn't the reason." Martha nodded. "I knew it was because she couldn't stand the silence in her house. Singing or humming was her way of keeping herself company."

A fat tear plopped onto the paper Trina was bending over. She was simultaneously relieved her mother had had someone like Martha in her life who understood her so well, yet saddened to be reminded of her mother's loneliness as a child. She might have started crying in earnest if Timothy and Tanner hadn't clomped into the room at just that moment.

Martha decided to lie down while Trina accompanied the boys to the basement. Largely empty, the room served as an ideal place for them to ride their bicycles—with training wheels attached—during inclement weather, but Trina liked to be present to make sure they didn't pedal too fast, since the floor was cement and she didn't want them getting hurt.

Much to Trina's relief, it was soon time to make supper. Seth had been right; after a full day of rain, she did feel cooped up. Also, although she'd never especially liked the constant noise and bustle of the city, she'd become accustomed to it, so it seemed strange not to see any people other than the Helmuth family for an entire week. Itching to get out and go shopping, she was eager for Seth to return. Admittedly, she was also curious about his trip to the matchmaker, but for his sake Trina hoped Martha wouldn't ask him about it during supper.

Seth's trip to see the matchmaker paid off quicker than he expected. Belinda suggested he consider courting Fannie Jantzi, a widow who lived just over the Elmsville town line. The matchmaker said Fannie was a pet project of hers and Seth didn't know if that was a good sign or a bad one. But when Belinda told him Fannie could be available the next day, Seth agreed to pick her up at a nearby phone shanty after their separate church services ended. Feeling hopeful, he hurried home to eat supper with Martha, Trina and the boys.

After taking a bite of bread, Seth set it aside on his plate. He had made leather purses that were probably easier to chew. Trina must have baked it. He tried to be discreet, but Tanner noticed he wasn't eating his slice.

"*Daed*, you have to tear into the bread with your teeth like this," he advised, showing what he meant. "Pretend you're a lion and it's carrion."

"That's enough, Tanner," Seth scolded, disconcerted. Trina appeared drained tonight as it was; he hoped she wasn't offended by Tanner's remark but he couldn't tell because she dipped her chin toward her chest. Then he noticed her shoulders shaking a little. Was she crying over such a small thing? But when she glanced up and swallowed a drink of water, he could see she was fighting laughter. He had to give it to her; she was awfully good-natured.

"Look, *Daed*, you can see two of yourselves in *Groossmammi*'s eyes," Timothy pointed out, waving to his reflection in Martha's glasses.

"Put your hand down and eat your vegetation." Seth had meant to say *vegetables* but he subconsciously adopted Trina's word choice. He'd been thinking about how he'd have to pick up a pair of less conspicuous sunglasses for Martha tonight. He was embarrassed he hadn't thought of buying her a pair earlier, but she'd never complained about the lighting before. Or was it that he'd never thought to ask? Once again, he was thankful for Trina's attentiveness to his family.

After they ate, Martha and Trina quickly cleared the table and washed the dishes while Seth and the boys hitched the horse and brought the buggy up the lane.

"I'll sit in the back with the *buwe* and Trina can sit up front with you," Martha said.

Inwardly Seth groaned. It would be difficult to conduct a conversation between the front and back seats, and he didn't know what to converse with Trina about on his own. He hoped the boys would call out their many questions, but instead, Martha engaged Timothy and Tanner in a spirited conversation about sheep shearing that Seth could barely hear from his seat in front.

"This is such fun!" Trina trilled, spreading the blanket Seth had given her over her lap.

Seth chuckled. "It's a mode of transportation, not a carnival ride." *Uh-oh, did that sound rude?* He actually thought her delight was charming, so he quickly added, "It's probably a big change from driving a car around Philadelphia."

"I wouldn't know about that," Trina said breezily. "I don't own a car."

"Then how do you get around? Bus? Train?"

"Sometimes, but mostly I walk. Or ride a bike."

"In Philadelphia?"

"It's a city, not the moon," she said, imitating his tone when he remarked about the buggy not being a carnival ride. Then she teased, "*Englischers* have feet, too, you know."

Seth chortled. "*Jah,* but do *Englischers* eat carrion for supper?"

Trina giggled. "I promise I didn't teach them that. I don't know where they learned it."

"From me." When Trina twisted sideways and looked at him in surprise, Seth added, "We see a lot of things when we're out walking in the countryside. Not all of it is pleasant, but it's a fact of life."

"The same might be said for walking in the city," Trina mumbled. There was a hint of sadness to her dulcet voice.

"Staying in Willow Creek must be a big adjustment for you."

"In some ways, *jah.* But my *mamm* told me so much about it when I was growing up it almost seems like I've been here before."

Now there was no mistaking her melancholy tone. "I'm sorry about your *mamm*," he said. "You may know this already, but the first year is the most difficult. The grief never goes away completely, but after a year, it changes. And with more time, it will change again. At least, that's how it was for me after I lost my Eleanor."

Ordinarily Seth wouldn't share such an intimate sentiment with an *Englisch* woman—or an Amish woman, for that matter. But Trina's voice carried such a note of fragility, he found himself wanting to comfort her.

"I do take comfort in knowing my *mamm* is with the Lord, but sometimes I'm unbearably lonely without her."

That was exactly how Seth felt. "*Jah*, if there was any consolation for me about Timothy and Tanner, it was that they never knew their *mamm,* so they didn't miss her the way I did. Even so, it's been hard on them not to have a *mamm* in their life."

"Oh, I see," Trina spoke quietly, presumably so the boys and Martha wouldn't hear her. "So that's why you visited the matchmaker today— you're ready to court again?"

Seth didn't feel comfortable continuing this conversation, but when he didn't respond, Trina assured him, "There's no need to be embarrassed. I've had friends who've tried online dating services and—"

"Ha!" Seth sputtered. "A matchmaker is nothing like an online dating service."

"How do you know?" Trina challenged. "Have you ever tried an online dating service?"

"Have you ever tried an Amish matchmaker?"

"*Neh*, but my *mamm* told me enough about them for me to know they're not so different from online dating services, especially from dating services that screen people to find out what their values, interests and hopes are. How is that so different from going to a matchmaker?"

"The very fact you call it *dating* shows the difference," Seth argued. "Courtships among the Amish are primarily intended to see if a couple is compatible for marriage. *Englischers* date for social entertainment."

"That's true for some *Englischers*, but not everyone dates casually. Some are very selective and when they enter a romantic relationship, it's with the hope of eventually marrying."

Seth didn't know how the conversation had jumped from talking about buggy rides to courtships and marriage—topics he would have been reluctant to discuss with his closest

Amish friends, much less with an *Englischer* he barely knew. But since she'd been so bold as to ask him about going to the matchmaker, he figured he could venture an inquiry, too. "Don't tell me, you're the kind of person who only dates with the intention of marrying?"

"Neh," Trina answered, the verve suddenly gone from her voice. "But I don't date for fun, either. I mean, there was someone I thought I'd marry, but…"

"But the dating service made a bad match?" Seth couldn't resist needling her a final time.

"I didn't meet him through a dating service." Trina seemed a million miles away when she said, "But you're right, he wasn't a *gut* match. He broke up with me when my *mamm* became ill. He said he couldn't compete with her for my time and affection."

Seth regretted bringing up such a painful subject. What kind of man wouldn't support the woman he loved when her mother had cancer? "What a self-centered *dummkopf*," he said aloud, answering his own question.

"It's better I found out sooner rather than later." Trina sounded genuinely sincere when she added, "But I hope things turn out well for you."

Trina was quiet the rest of the way to Highland Springs and Seth felt terrible for spoiling what had started out as such a fun excursion for her. Once they arrived at the store, he and Martha took Timothy and Tanner with them, despite the boys' expressed preference for accompanying Trina. Seth figured she needed time to collect her items in peace, and besides, he didn't want to mar her evening further by making any more cloddish remarks.

Trina was relieved when Sunday came; it meant she'd made it through one week in Willow Creek. Only a little more than eight weeks to go until May first. She rose early to attend the nearest *Englisch* church, which, according to the map on her phone, was two and a half miles away. Since she didn't have a car and couldn't afford to hire a taxi to come from Lancaster, she had to walk. On the way, she hummed as she thought about Seth, Martha and the boys traveling to the worship services hosted this week by an Amish family, the Planks.

The sky was overcast with white clouds and Trina hoped the light wasn't bothering Martha's eyes. Seth had bought his grandmother a new pair of sunglasses the evening before, but they didn't fit over Martha's regular glasses as well as the pair she'd borrowed from Trina. When Trina told Martha she should consider going to an eye doctor and getting prescription sunglasses, Seth said he doubted that was necessary and Martha seemed to agree. Trina was puzzled by this; they didn't seem excessively frugal, but she supposed they might have considered the expense to be a waste.

Because it was chillier than Trina expected and she hadn't worn a hat, halfway to church she stopped and let her hair down from its ponytail so it would provide a natural covering for her ears. Fortunately there was no wind as she trod up and down the hilly roads of Willow Creek, but by the time she arrived at the little church and ducked into the women's room, her nose and cheeks were bright pink, and she felt famished from hiking in the cold. She ran her hands under warm water and then joined the small but friendly congregation. The pastor's sermon on God's faithfulness was comforting to her and she especially loved worshipping through song. She hadn't realized until today how long it had been since she was able to sing in church; ever since her mother died, she was afraid to lift up her voice, in fear she'd begin crying in public. But today she sang as loudly and cheerfully as anyone.

After the service, the elderly couple sitting next to Trina turned to introduce themselves to her as Sherman and Mabel Brown. They were delighted to learn she was new in town and they quickly invited her to the potluck dinner being held in the basement of the building. Trina's stomach rumbled as she accepted their offer.

She was eating her second plate of spaghetti and meatballs when a young man approached the table where Sherman and Mabel had introduced her to another couple with two children. The man took a seat next to Trina. Dark-haired and soft-spoken, Ethan Gray told her he was the local pediatrician. Like Trina, he'd only arrived in Willow Creek recently. After dessert—Trina had both a cupcake *and* a brownie—Ethan offered to give her a ride home, but Trina declined. Warm and invigorated again, she wanted to see Wheeler's Bridge, which was located not too far from Main Street. Trina's mother had told her that when she went grocery shopping in town as a girl, instead of walking on the roads she always followed the creek behind their house all the way to the bridge. She said the route took her through the thick woods and beautiful Amish farmland, so Trina was eager to journey where her mother had once found beauty.

Following the directions on her phone's GPS, Trina had been walking for almost half an hour when it began drizzling. Within minutes, she felt the prickle of sleet against her scalp and she dashed to take cover beneath a willow tree in the middle of a field. Since the tree had no foliage yet, it provided little shelter and Trina's hair became ropy and wet as she consulted her phone to figure out a shortcut home. She concluded if she cut across the field she was standing in and took a short jaunt through a wooded area, she'd wind up on a street that ran parallel to Main Street. Since it was the Sabbath, the Amish shops were closed, but she hoped there would be a convenience store or a coffee shop she could stop in at to dry off and get a hot chocolate.

But she must have gotten confused in the woods because when she finally emerged some forty minutes later, she recognized the fence as being the same one that bordered the east end of the field where she first began. Or was it? There were so many fences and farms in Willow Creek it was difficult to distinguish one from another. And since the trees and hills hadn't yet begun to show signs of spring, it wasn't even as if the walk had been especially scenic. Worst of all, by now it was raining so hard it was soaking right through her jacket. Trina had no choice but to use her phone to navigate along the roads instead of taking a shortcut.

By that time, she'd been walking for over

an hour, her toes were numb and she wished she'd accepted a ride from Ethan. She was half tempted to flag down a passing car, except that no cars passed her. She had just trudged up a long, steep hill when her phone rang. It had been so long since she'd received a phone call, she jerked when it vibrated in her pocket.

"Hello?" she answered, pushing a string of wet hair from her eyes. Droplets rolled off her eyebrows and she squinted against the rain.

The caller, Kurt Johnson, explained he was a realtor who'd heard she had a small house that might be for sale. *Who could have told him that?* she wondered. Kurt asked if they could meet soon. Just then, a car came over the hill at a high speed, its wheels spraying Trina with dirt and mud as it passed.

"Oh, no!" she wailed.

"I'm sorry?" Kurt asked.

"Nothing," Trina replied. "Listen, this isn't a *gut* time—a good time—for me to talk. Try again later, okay? I have to go. Bye." Hanging up before he could say anything else, Trina felt kind of rude but she didn't think it was very polite of him to call her on a Sunday, either.

Great, she thought, looking down. *Now this skirt is muddy and I haven't even washed the other one yet. Can this excursion possibly get any worse?*

* * *

As Seth crested the hill, he saw a flash of lavender on the descending side. Only one person he knew wore a jacket that color: Trina. Her dark hair was plastered to her head as she stood on the roadside four miles from home, talking on a cell phone in the pouring rain.

"Narrish Englischer." Seated next to him, Fannie said aloud what Seth was thinking: Trina was a crazy *Englischer.* But she was also his boys' nanny. And she was extremely wet. So, despite the fact he was technically courting Fannie—really he was just taking her to his home for a Sunday afternoon visit—he knew he had to stop and offer Trina a ride. The very last thing he wanted to do.

"Why are you pulling over?" Fannie questioned after they passed Trina by several yards and he had time and room to halt the horse and buggy.

"That's my *buwe*'s nanny. She lives next door to me. I'm sorry but I have to see if she needs a ride."

Fannie's brown eyes bulged with surprise. "An *Englisch* nanny takes care of your *kinner*? No wonder you're eager to marry again!"

Seth's own eyes widened at her comment. It seemed a brash thing for her to say, considering they'd only just met, but he recognized there was truth to her remark. Like him, Fannie had two young children and was eager to wed.

"You're bringing a woman to our house?" Martha had asked the previous night after they returned from the market and Timothy and Tanner were in bed. "Do you think that's a *gut* idea?"

"Why not? I need to find out how she gets along with the *buwe*. And with you."

Martha shook her head. "I'm not the one courting her. Neither are the *buwe*. And I dare say you won't be for long, either, if your idea of courtship is to bring her home and test her compatibility with the *kinner* and me. Besides, I didn't even make a dessert."

Seth was stumped by Martha's remarks. He and Fannie weren't youth; they'd both been married before, and according to Belinda, their shared objective in courting again was to find a suitable parent for their children as well as a spouse. If things went well today, he fully intended to meet Fannie's daughters next Sunday. He hadn't, however, intended for Fannie to meet Trina. Certainly not today and possibly not at all.

Sighing, he hopped down from the buggy. "What are you doing out here?" he asked when Trina approached.

She put her hand to her forehead as if to shield her eyes from the sun, but clearly it was the rain she didn't want interfering with her vision. "Am I ever glad to see you!" she explained. "I'm lost. I was trying to—"

She looked so bedraggled and worn out that Seth cut her off. "Never mind. You can tell me in the buggy. You'll have to sit in the back."

After Trina was seated and Seth had made introductions, Trina apologized for interrupting their afternoon. Her teeth chattered as she spoke, but she projected her voice so they could hear her. "I was coming home from church when the skies opened up. I started out by using my GPS but then I thought I'd figured out a shortcut through the woods, but I must have gotten all turned around because I ended up back where I started."

"It must be so difficult when you have to rely on technology to get where you need to go," Fannie said over her shoulder and clicked her tongue against her teeth.

Seth couldn't tell whether her comment was meant as sympathy or criticism, but suddenly he found himself defending Trina. "She wasn't using technology to get where she wanted to go—she was using her feet. Which is more than you and I are doing."

Fannie cracked up, as if he'd intended to

amuse her. "*Lappich!* I wasn't talking about her transportation. I was talking about using her cell phone to figure out where to go."

"Actually," Trina countered, "I rarely use GPS and I wouldn't have used it today but I didn't have a map, I'm new in town and I really didn't want to miss church. Besides, it's not the GPS that failed me. It was my own sense of direction I was following through the woods."

"What church did you go to?" Seth asked and when Trina replied, he whistled. "You must have walked a *gut* three miles to end up where you are now. It's another three miles home."

"Wow, I really did go out of my way. The church was only two and a half miles from my house when I started out this morning," she joked.

"Either that or the road grew longer while you were in church," Seth teased. "That must have been some lengthy sermon!"

Trina giggled but Fannie shook her head. "I don't think it's proper to joke about worship," she said under her breath and then was silent for the rest of the trip.

"*Denki* for the ride," Trina said to Seth when he dropped her off at her house. Then she told Fannie it was nice to meet her.

As Trina climbed the steps to her door, Fannie remarked, "The poor thing, her husband is going to think she looks like something the *katz* dragged in."

"She doesn't have a husband."

"Ah. I wondered about that."

Seth didn't know what she was getting at. "Why would you wonder about whether Trina has a husband or not?"

"Oh, just because she went to church alone," Fannie said. Then, before Seth could offer to drop her off at his front door, she asked, "Could you let me off here? I'll get wet walking from the stable and since your buggy doesn't have a heater, I'm already cold."

Once again, Seth couldn't tell if she was being critical. Their *Ordnung* allowed certain kinds of heaters in their buggies, but he felt blankets worked just fine for the short distances they usually traveled. Would Fannie expect him to get a heater while they were courting? His mind jumped to Trina's remarks about how much fun it was to ride in the buggy the previous night. Then he realized Trina hadn't complained at all about being cold on the way home today, even though Fannie had two blankets on her lap and Trina had had none. Seth shook his head and told himself he was probably the one being critical about Fannie. *I need to see how she interacts with the* buwe *and* Groossmammi *before I make any quick judgments,* he thought.

When Seth returned from the stable Fannie was already in the parlor with Martha and the boys, sitting next to the woodstove. "Have you met everyone, Fannie?" he asked.

"*Jah*. Your *groossmammi* and I thought we'd have tea as soon as my feet warm up, and then Timothy and Turner are going to show me how they play a game called Noah's Ark."

"You mean Tanner," Tanner told her.

"What?" Fannie asked.

"My name is Tanner. You called me Turner."

"Oh, did I?" Fannie asked. "That's probably because you've been spinning in so many circles since I arrived, I thought your name was Turner."

"I can spin, too!" Timothy announced, showing them.

"I'll say you can," Fannie agreed. "You can spin just like a tornado. I should call you Twister. Turner and Twister."

The boys' laughter allayed some of Seth's reservations and he offered to get the tea.

"Nonsense," Fannie objected. When Martha rose from her chair, Fannie said, "I'll make it. Martha, you just stay put. This will give me a chance to familiarize myself with your kitchen."

If there was one thing that nettled Seth's grandmother more than anything else, it was having another woman in her kitchen. It didn't matter that Martha was nearly blind; she was in charge of her kitchen and that was that. In fact, it had surprised Seth when his grandmother allowed Trina to make suppers, but he assumed it was because Martha was teaching her to become a better cook. In any case, Seth held his breath, waiting to see how his grandmother would react to Fannie saying she'd get the tea.

"Denki," Martha finally replied, lowering herself into the chair again. "That would be *wunderbaar."*

Seth exhaled and sat down at the end of the sofa.

"Seth," his grandmother whispered loudly and gestured toward his head. "Your *hut*. Take off your *hut*."

Seth chuckled. He'd forgotten to remove it. As he went to hang it on a peg, he smoothed his hair. It was damp near the back of his neck, but not nearly as wet as Trina's had been.

Poor maedel, *she must be chilled to the bone,* he thought. *I hope she remembers how I showed her to build a fire. Maybe I'll have time to check before I take Fannie back to her home.*

Then he thought better of it. Fannie seemed

to disapprove of *Englischers* even more than Seth sometimes did and he sensed she didn't think it was appropriate for him to be so concerned about Trina. He supposed Fannie was right. Trina wasn't his responsibility. He had a courtship to pursue, if not with Fannie—he still wasn't sure what he thought about her—then with another Amish woman Belinda would introduce him to. So he returned to the parlor and joined Martha and Fannie as the boys showed them the game their *Englisch* nanny had taught them.

Chapter Four

After Seth left the house on Monday, Tanner and Timothy filled Trina in about Seth's afternoon with Fannie. Although Trina hadn't prompted them, she was curious about what kind of woman Fannie was. Trina's initial impression was that she was a little uptight, but that might have been because it was her first time out with Seth and she was nervous.

"Yesterday we showed *Daed* and Fannie how to play Noah's Ark," Timothy told Trina as they walked along the bank of the creek. Just as Trina expected, once Seth saw how closely she kept watch over his sons, he'd allowed the trio to trek along their favorite path.

"That must have been fun," Trina replied, pleased they liked the game enough to show it to their father.

"It wasn't as much fun as with you. Fannie couldn't guess we were being inchworms," Tanner complained.

"We did this," Timothy said. He imitated an inchworm alternately raising itself into an arch with its hind legs and advancing forward with its front legs until it was stretched flat again.

Trina clapped, laughing. "That was excellent, Timothy!" The child had really captured the essence of an inchworm's movements. The boys had probably studied the little critters on one of their countryside walks with Seth.

"Fannie didn't think so. She thought I was being a camel."

"Maybe she thought you were making your back into a hump, like a camel's." Even as she offered the diplomatic explanation, Trina wondered how Fannie could have mistaken Timothy's movements for anything other than an inchworm. The imitation was so accurate it didn't take much imagination to guess what he was doing. "Did your *daed* guess?"

"*Neh*, he said 'ladies first,' so Fannie kept guessing and guessing and she didn't ever give him a turn. Then Tanner told her we being were inchworms."

"She was taking too long and I wanted us to be bears, instead," Tanner said.

Trina tried not to giggle. That was exactly how Fannie had struck her, as someone who didn't easily admit defeat. Not that it mattered much to Trina. Seth was the one who'd have to figure out if she was a "*gut* match" for him or not. Trina said, "Well, I think it was kind of you to show Fannie the game. In time, she'll learn how to play."

"*Jah*, like you and the *oier*," Tanner said, stopping to toss a rock into the creek.

"What do you mean, like me and the *oier*?" Trina asked.

"*Daed* said *Englischers* collect their *oier* from a grocery store and it's not nice to laugh if you're scared of the *hinkel*. In time you'll collect *oier* from the henhouse, too."

Trina didn't know whether she felt indignant or grateful for Seth's instruction to the boys. Yes, he was teaching Timothy and Tanner to demonstrate kindness, but he was also emphasizing her difference. "Your *Daed* is right. I will learn to collect *oier* from the henhouse. In fact, I'm going to collect them from now on, without any help from you *buwe*."

"Aw, but we like to help you, Trina." Tanner stomped on a fallen pine cone.

"You can still help. You'll hold the basket for me."

Indeed, the next day, Trina retrieved the eggs on her own. One broody hen didn't want to relinquish her spot in the nesting box, but

Trina successfully shoed her away on the second try. She placed the warm brown eggs in the basket Tanner held out for her and then Timothy carried it into the house.

Martha had planned to use a couple of the eggs to make custard pie for her friends, Pearl Hostetler, Ruth Graber and Ruth's daughter-in-law, Iris. They were coming to work on one of the quilts they donated to a charity for children in foster care. But after dinner Martha's eyes were bothering her so much she developed a headache and had to lie down.

"Ruth will probably bring a treat from her nephew's wife's bakery anyway," Martha said.

Trina had heard about the renowned treats Faith Schwartz made and she hoped she'd get a chance to visit the bakery. She was amazed by how voracious her appetite was lately; it was as if she was making up for all the months she'd subsisted on nothing but fruit and crackers or bread.

Once she put the boys down for a nap, Trina decided to bake something on Martha's behalf, in case Ruth showed up empty-handed. While she didn't know how to make custard pie without a recipe, her mother had taught her to bake funny cake—a popular Amish dessert that was a cross between a coffee cake and a chocolate pie. *I might be new to collecting* oier, *but I'm no stranger to rolling a pie crust,* she thought as she worked the dough.

Knowing the boys would want a piece, she doubled the recipe and she was pulling the second pie from the oven when Martha meandered into the room, sniffing.

"That smells *appenditlich*. Is it cake?"

"*Jah,* it's funny cake. You have a *gut* sense of smell."

"Not half as *gut* as Seth and his *seh*. They can smell dessert a mile away. I'm surprised Timothy and Tanner haven't *kumme* running."

"They're napping—"

Trina was interrupted by someone tapping the windowpane on the door.

"*Wilkom,*" Martha said as she ushered her guests inside. "*Kumme,* meet Trina Smith, Patience Kauffman's *dochder*."

"Look at you! You're the image of your *mamm* at your age, isn't she, Ruth?" Pearl asked.

"*Jah*, she is. She is, indeed," the other elderly woman agreed. She pulled Trina close and kissed her cheek, whispering, "May *Gott* comfort you in your grief."

"*Denki*. He already is," Trina whispered back.

Moved by the warm reception she'd received, Trina offered to make tea for the three older women and Iris, who looked to be about Trina's mother's age.

"That's a *gut* idea. Let's have dessert while it's warm before you take out your material and supplies. Go ahead into the parlor, we'll be there in a minute," Martha directed.

Trina accepted when Martha offered her assistance. She knew nothing bothered Martha as much as being treated as if she were incapable of helping, especially in her own kitchen.

"There are only four slices here," Martha said, holding the tray. "Where's yours?"

Trina didn't expect to be invited to join the group. "The *buwe* will be awake soon, so—"

"So you'd better cut yourself a slice and *kumme* sit down before they do."

Trina couldn't argue with Martha any more than Seth could, so she obediently cut herself a piece of the funny cake and went into the parlor, too.

"Mm-mmm!" Ruth murmured. "You outdid yourself this time, Martha. I intended to stop by the bakery to get sweets for us, but now I'm glad I didn't."

"I wish I could say it's mine but Trina made it with no help from me."

"This crust…" Iris began to say but finished chewing and swallowing before she continued "…is so flaky. What's your secret?"

"Denki," Trina answered demurely. "My *mamm* taught me how to make it."

"Ah, then, you're not going to tell us your secret, are you?" Ruth winked at her and turned to Pearl. "Remember how Patience would never tell us the secret, either?"

"Jah, all she ever said was her *mamm* taught *her*!" Pearl laughed. "No matter how often we pleaded, she didn't give in. In the end, we decided we'd rather eat it than make it anyway, and we quit pestering her."

Trina giggled. Her mother had told her that the secret—which involved working the dough and using baking powder—was something that had been passed down for generations. It was such a comfort to hear the women share their recollections of her mother that Trina was sorry when the boys woke up.

She allowed each to eat a slender slice of cake in the kitchen before taking them outdoors. As she was lacing Tanner's boots for him, she overheard Pearl ask Martha about Seth's afternoon with Fannie. Trina's mother was right; she always said there were no secrets in Willow Creek—except for recipes, perhaps. Trina strained to hear Martha's reply.

"I can't tell if Seth thought she was a *gut* match or not, although who knows what that *bu* is looking for."

"What about you, what did you think?" Ruth asked.

"She took over my kitchen!" Martha replied frankly and Trina could hear the others gasp in exaggerated horror before bursting into laughter.

While she knew it was uncharitable of her, Trina would be lying if she said she wasn't a tiny bit glad neither Martha nor the boys took a liking to Fannie. And, although she couldn't say why for certain she felt this way, she was even happier Seth didn't seem crazy about her, either.

As Seth clomped up the porch stairs the smell of something delicious tickled his nostrils. He only had to open the door before he identified the aroma: funny cake. Martha hadn't made that in over a year.

"Martha? Trina? *Buwe?*" he called, but no one answered. The table was set and stew was simmering on the stovetop, so they couldn't have gone far. He lifted the plastic wrap off the pie plate. A little slice wouldn't ruin his appetite.

"*Daed,* no sweets before supper," Tanner scolded when he, Timothy and Trina came upstairs from the basement and caught Seth devouring his second piece over the sink without using a plate.

"I couldn't resist," Seth explained to Trina. "Martha hasn't made this in years. She sure hasn't lost her touch, though."

Timothy corrected him. "*Groossmammi* didn't make that cake. Trina did."

"*Jah*, with *oier* she collected all by herself."

"Please go wash your hands," Trina instructed the boys, who charged from the room.

Chagrinned, Seth clapped the crumbs from his hands. "It really is *gut*. So, did giving you baking lessons wear my *groossmammi* out? Or is she lying down because she has a *koppweh*?"

"*Neh*, she went with her friends to deliver the quilts to the charity. She'll be back soon." Trina moved toward him to wash her hands at the sink. "By the way, Martha didn't teach me how to make a funny cake—my *mamm* did."

"Oh, sorry about that," Seth apologized. In an attempt to make up for his blunder, he added, "I'm sorry the *buwe* didn't help you at the henhouse, too. I'll talk to them tonight."

Trina's tone was smug. "No need to apologize—I wanted to collect the *oier* myself."

Seth's voice cracked with disbelief when he asked, "You did?"

This time Trina laughed. "It's not all that much different than sticking my hand into a refrigerator at a grocery store and pulling out a carton of eggs like we *Englischers* all do, is it?"

"I admit, I'm impressed by your progress," Seth replied, leaning toward her and grinning. "Next thing you know, you won't need me to help you catch mice, either."

Trina's eyes were so sincerely fearful as she said, "Please don't make me do that myself," that Seth had the impulse to tousle her hair in consolation, the way he might do to the boys.

Instead he said, "On one condition. You make another funny cake again soon. This one is almost gone."

She ribbed him, saying, "Hmm, I wonder why. But okay, it's a deal." She thrust her hand out to shake his but then she suddenly dropped it to her side. "Sorry. That's an *Englisch* habit."

He lifted her hand in his anyway, peered into her dancing green eyes and said, "Deal."

True to her word, the following Saturday morning, Trina showed up bearing a pie plate covered in foil. "I think I heard the trap snap last night. Will you check it for me?"

Seth guffawed. "I wasn't serious about the cake but *jah*, I'll go check the trap."

When he returned a few minutes later, Timothy and Tanner were waiting for him on the porch. "*Daed*, Trina says we have to ask you if we can have a piece of your cake."

"*Jah*, but not until after your afternoon nap," he answered. Then he told Trina he'd emptied the trap. Now that the mouse was out of the wall, he could patch the crack, but he'd have to wait until he returned from work around two thirty or three o'clock before he could get to it.

"I wouldn't mind taking a piece of that cake with me, though," he said, and she cut him a generous slice.

Just the thought of it made his mouth water and he looked forward to eating it during his break, but at noon Joseph Schrock, the owner of Schrock's Shop a few doors down Main Street, stopped in to visit.

"Have you heard the news? It's *baremlich*, isn't it?" the bespectacled man asked.

"What news?"

"About Abe Kauffman's property."

Joseph proceeded to tell Seth a developer was interested in buying it once Trina met the requirements to sell. Apparently, after several failed attempts to reach Trina at home, the realtor stopped by Joseph's shop and inquired about her. He was excited to tell Joseph he had an investor who wanted to buy the property— not for the house, but for the land. The client's intention was to raze the house and build a beer, wine and spirits store there, since Willow Creek didn't have one on that side of town. He said with so many buses coming through Main Street, tourists would be thrilled to frequent a liquor store nearby. As a nod to local history, the shop would specialize in German beer and hard cider.

"A liquor store?" Seth echoed. He couldn't believe his ears. What could be worse than living next door to a liquor store? The traffic, the parking lot, the noise, the lighting…how was he going to raise two boys next to a business like that?

He was so discouraged he left his dinner uneaten and brooded for the afternoon, hardly able to concentrate on his customers' questions. To him the *Englischers* seemed unnecessarily preoccupied with the colors of the purses and wallets he made. As long as they securely held money, how much did the color matter? It was a frivolous concern, just like building a beer, wine and spirits store next door to him was an unnecessary pursuit.

It never occurred to him Trina wouldn't sell—she'd made it crystal clear she was leaving in two months. But Seth wondered if she could be persuaded not to sell to that particular developer. Perhaps she'd be willing to sell to an Amish family or at least to an *Englisch* family instead of a business. By the end of the day, he felt more hopeful and he polished off his lunch, funny cake and all, before walking home.

"*Buwe,* you stay here with *Groossmammi,*" he told Timothy and Tanner when he got there. He hoped to talk to Trina about the rumor he'd heard and he didn't want the boys listening.

"How was your day? Did you have a lot of customers?" she asked as they strolled across the yard to her house so he could take care of the crack in the wall.

"There was a steady stream, *jah.*"

"What kind of leatherwork do you sell in your shop?"

"My general inventory includes purses, harnesses, belts, tool pouches, that kind of thing. But often *Englisch* customers ask me to custom design something special. As long as it's made of leather, I can probably honor their request. Except for shoes or boots. I don't make those."

"Why not?"

She's certainly inquisitive today. Seth explained, "Usually the people who want me to custom design footwear for them want it because they can't find their size in a regular store. So if I make shoes for them and they change their minds, I'm stuck with a size fourteen boot. Or a double-wide size eight shoe. Those are hard to sell."

"Have you ever considered making them pay up front?" Trina asked as she opened her kitchen door.

"*Neh*. I believe people should be true to their word," Seth said, following her inside. "The problem is, the *Englisch* don't."

Trina twirled around so abruptly Seth didn't have time to stop walking and he almost bumped into her. She was nearly as tall as he was and they were so close he could see each individual lash on her lower eyelid. "I'm *Englisch* and I honor my word," she said, narrowing her eyes.

Seth didn't mean for another one of their conversations to become contentious, but with her standing so near, he couldn't think of what to say to fix it. Nor did he want to move away. "I—I…" he stammered.

Trina stepped backward and giggled. Oh, so she was only pretending to be angry. "Now it's your turn to honor *your* word." She gestured toward the kitchen cupboard.

Seth could feel his lips lift into a goofy smile but he didn't respond aloud. The tension between them was broken but it took him a moment to recover before he began patching the crack inside the cupboard. As he worked, Trina put on a pot for tea and he was almost ready to sit down and share a cup with her when someone knocked at the door.

"Yes?" Trina questioned after opening it.

"I'm Kurt Johnson," the short man with unusually bright teeth said. "You know, the realtor who called you last week. We talked about getting together, remember?"

So Trina had already been in touch with him. How could she have agreed to meet with someone who was going to sell to a developer? Didn't she understand what living next door to a liquor store would be like for Seth and his family—especially the boys?

"Sorry. I'd forgotten," Trina replied. "Um, this is my...my neighbor, Seth Helmuth."

Seth nodded and then turned his attention to collecting his tools.

"We were just about to sit down for tea. You're *wilkom* to join us," Trina said.

"Terrific!" Kurt seemed overly zealous to Seth.

"I'm actually heading home now," Seth told Trina. If she was going to make a deal with someone like Kurt, he didn't want to be there to bear witness to it.

Trina was disappointed when Seth left, but she didn't blame him; he probably thought

Kurt was a pushy *Englischer*—and he was right. From the moment he sat down until the moment Trina ushered him out the door, the realtor tried to convince Trina it was in her best interest to sell the property to a developer who wanted to use the land for commercial purposes. Specifically, to build a liquor store. When Trina heard that, she nearly choked on her tea.

"You'd be doing the community a service," he said. "And you'd stand to profit so much more than if you sold this house to a family."

"This community is Amish. They wouldn't patronize a liquor store," Trina replied. "And you still haven't told me how you knew my house might be for sale."

Kurt shrugged. "We have our ways of finding out. Now listen, even if the Amish won't patronize the shop, the tourists and non-Amish locals will. Indirectly, you'll be helping the Amish businesses flourish because it's only a tiny detour from Main Street to here. Business for the liquor store means business for the Amish shops and vice versa."

Trina shook her head. "I'm not selling to a developer. They'd ruin the land. There's a beautiful creek out back. The two *buwe*—I mean boys—living next door love to play out there. They won't be able to if cars are constantly driving in and out."

"You're being sentimental. This lot could command almost half a mil," Kurt said. "If you sell the house and land as-is for someone to reside in, you won't even see six figures."

Even five figures would have felt like a windfall to Trina, but that was beside the point. Trina absolutely wouldn't do that to the people of Willow Creek—especially the Helmuths. Besides, it would dishonor her mother's memory to allow the location to be used for a liquor store when alcohol had played such a detrimental role in her childhood.

Standing, Trina said, "I appreciate your input, but I have things to do." She had really hoped to get into town, since she was itching to see Main Street, but now it was too late, so she'd probably just do her laundry and then read.

"Alright. Here's my card if you have any questions. When can I stop in and see that you've changed your mind?"

"Never," Trina blurted out. "I mean, I'd prefer you call instead of stopping in. I'll give you my cell phone number."

"Already have it, remember?" Kurt held up his phone to show her. "And before you ask how I got it—"

"I know, I know. You have your ways," Trina said and Kurt gave her a cheesy grin.

After realizing she still had one clean skirt to wear to church the next day, Trina decided to forego washing her clothes until Monday, when she could hang them on the line first thing in the morning. Instead she ate a bowl of chili and curled up with a book Martha had loaned her, followed by studying the Bible in preparation for church.

Stretching out in bed that night, she felt toasty warm and thought of her mother. Trina wished she had a photo of her when she was a girl, but of course, photos were prohibited among the Amish. She loved it whenever people said she looked like her mother, although Trina thought Patience had been far prettier than Trina would ever be. Then she found herself wondering what Seth's wife must have looked like, since the boys looked exactly like him.

More and more her thoughts turned to Seth lately. Instead of being annoyed when he teased her about the *Englisch*, she enjoyed being the focus of his attention and she rather liked teasing him back. She thought of how close their faces had been this afternoon and she shivered. What was wrong with her? Did she have a crush on him, or was it simply that he was one of the only two adults she spoke to on a regular basis? As she rolled onto her side and adjusted her pillow beneath her neck, she anticipated going to church would help refocus her thoughts.

Indeed, the next day Trina's mind was wholly occupied with the pastor's sermon and with singing praises to the Lord. Once again, after the service ended Ethan offered her a ride home, and once again she declined. She was sure she could make it to Main Street today. Even though the stores were all closed, she could peek into the shop windows. The mercantile and Schrock's Shop were the only stores she remembered her mother mentioning; the bakery, seasonal ice cream parlor, and furniture restoration shop must have been new since her mother was a girl.

Also, there was Seth's leather shop. Or, as the plain sign said: Helmuth's Leatherworks. Trina peeked in the large glass window. The storefront wasn't as large as she expected, but she remembered Seth saying most of the space was dedicated to his workshop, which was located in the back of the store. Even from a distance she could see how beautiful his handiwork was and she felt a sense of admiration. You couldn't buy such finely crafted items in the most extravagant *Englisch* shop in Philadelphia.

From there, she walked to Wheeler's Bridge and Wheeler's Pond, which had a few slushy ice chunks floating in it but otherwise wasn't frozen over. This was where her mother used to go skating with her friends. She remembered her mother telling her how, on her thirteenth birthday, she and her friend Katrina spent the afternoon skating there and then Katrina's mother had brought the girls home for hot chocolate and whoopie pies, Patience's favorite. Trina was filled with happiness at seeing these sights and she practically pranced home.

The creek meandered behind several houses and when she spotted a few Amish farmers or Amish children, she worried they'd forbid her to trespass, but they merely waved and she waved back. Finally, just as she was climbing the hill leading home, she saw Timothy and Tanner, and her heart skipped a beat as she imagined Seth was close by. But no, it was Martha sitting on a rock, her face turned toward the sun. They must have finished their family's worship services, since it was an *off Sunday*, meaning Amish families gathered separately in their own homes instead of as a community.

"*Guder nammidaag*, Martha!" Trina called. Martha waved in her direction and the boys darted straight for her, each trying to outrun the other. Tanner won.

"I prayed we'd see you today," he said after he caught his breath.

"Me, too," Timothy echoed.

Trina's heart absolutely swelled with affection.

"Specially 'cause we asked *Daed* if you could *kumme* to our house for worship but he said *neh*."

"*Jah*, he said you're *Englisch* and you go to an *Englisch* church and you're like a puppy."

"A puppy?" Trina questioned as the threesome trod toward Martha.

"*Jah*. We found a lost puppy and we wanted to keep it but *Groossmammi* is 'lergic. *Daed* said not to get too close to you or we'll be sad, like we were about giving away the puppy."

"Am I too close to you now, Trina?" Timothy asked, taking a step away from her.

Now Trina was angry. It was one thing when Seth teased her about her *Englisch* ways; she enjoyed their banter. But it was another thing altogether to point out her differences to the boys and make them afraid to be near her. Didn't he know how children took language literally at this age?

"*Neh*, you're not close enough," she said,

squatting down and holding her arms wide. "*Kumme* closer and give me a hug."

Both Tanner and Timothy squeezed closer, nearly knocking her over. She hugged them tightly and then let go. "Now, did that make you sad?" she asked.

"*Neh*," they answered in unison.

"Then I guess I'm not like that stray puppy, after all, am I?"

"*Neh*, a puppy goes like this." Timothy scooted away, barking, and his brother pretended to wag his tail as he followed.

"Give me your arm, dear," Martha said when Trina reached her, and Trina steadied her as they walked home behind the boys. Trina's cheeks were stinging, but it wasn't from the cold. She was so distraught over Seth's remarks she could barely manage one-word replies to Martha's questions about church.

Finally the old woman stopped and said, "Please don't mind the *buwe*'s comments. I heard what they told you and that's not exactly how Seth explained the differences to them."

"But it's the gist, I'm sure," Trina said sharply, not even censoring her anger for Martha.

"Perhaps, but you have to understand. He's actually trying to protect the *buwe*."

Trina dropped Martha's arm. "Protect them?

From *me*? If I'm so dangerous, why is he allowing me to watch Timothy and Tanner at all?"

"Ach, I've said the wrong thing," Martha muttered and her eyes filled. "I didn't mean you were dangerous. I meant...you see, Seth's brother, Freeman, fell in love with an *Englischer*. She promised she intended to join the Amish and she lived with an Amish family not far from here for almost two years in preparation. But in the end, she couldn't give up her *Englisch* lifestyle, so Freeman gave up his Amish one."

Trina took Martha's arm again, feeling guilty, as Martha continued speaking.

"It broke Seth's *mamm*'s heart and she died shortly after. Seth's *daed* had died years before, so Seth was left alone. I don't know if he's ever forgiven Freeman or his wife. I think he carries a lot of fear and hurt, which manifest as intolerance. No matter what Freeman chose, I know Seth still loves and misses his brother. I think he wants to be sure the *buwe* don't miss you like that when you leave. That's what I meant by protecting them."

Trina felt the anxiety dissolve from her body. "*Denki*, Martha, for telling me that. It helps." Then she laughed. "I guess I am kind of a stray, aren't I?"

"Neh!" Martha vehemently denied it. "You're a gift from *Gott* to our family."

"So is your family to me," Trina said, patting Martha's arm. She was assisting the older woman up the stairs to her home as Seth exited the house. The bright blue collar of his good church shirt turned his eyes from steely gray to bright blue and his honeyed hair shone in the sunlight before he set his hat on his head.

"Guder nammidaag, Trina," he said tersely before turning to Martha. "I'll see you this evening. Don't keep supper for me."

When he was out of earshot, Martha whispered, "He's going courting again."

Even though Trina had expected as much, her heart sank as she led Martha inside for tea.

On his way to Fannie's house, Seth thought more about Trina than he did about Fannie. He kept wondering what she'd told the realtor. He could only hope she hadn't made any decisions, because he wanted to talk to her first. Maybe if he presented his case, or if he found a family who was looking for a new place to live, he could get her to change her mind.

With those thoughts preoccupying him, he arrived at Fannie's house. Her two girls, Greta and Hope, ages five and eight, respectively, greeted him in the yard as he was hitching his horse to the post. They led him inside, where Fannie was preparing a tray of dessert with coffee for the adults and hot chocolate for the children. Seth was a little taken aback when each of the girls helped themselves to two thimble cookies and a honey bar each before Fannie even set the tray on the coffee table in the parlor. A few minutes later the girls discarded the treats, half eaten.

When he and Fannie finished theirs, he suggested, "Why don't we go for a walk? It's unusually sunny and warm outside today."

But Hope whined about wanting to play a game of Go Fish. Apparently, Fannie had promised her they'd play together. Before the end of the game, Greta was in tears because she lost, and Hope and Fannie were arguing over whether Hope peeked at her mother's cards. Seth was glad when they'd eaten supper—or, in the girls' case, had eaten half their suppers—and he could head home. He'd already decided to ask Belinda to introduce him to someone else.

Martha had managed to put the boys to bed herself and she was waiting for him in the parlor. "So, how was your afternoon with Fannie and her *dechder*?"

When he finished telling her about the game and the desserts, Martha clicked her tongue. "I guess it's not just the *Englisch* who spoil their *kinner,* after all, is it?"

Seth realized she was referencing remarks he sometimes made about *Englisch* customers. "*Jah*, you're right. But the Amish would never build a liquor store next door to us." Then he told Martha what Joseph had told him, peppering the conversation with references to the realtor as "a little weasel."

"I'm sure Trina would never sell her *mamm*'s house to a developer for a wine and spirits shop," she said dismissively.

"How do you know that?"

"Because I knew her *mamm* and she didn't raise a *dochder* like that."

"How can you say that?" Seth asked incredulously. "Her *mamm* left the Amish! She became an *Englischer.* She abandoned her *daed*! You can't trust—"

"Listen here, young man," Martha interrupted. "You don't know what you're talking about. Trina's *mamm* didn't abandon her *daed*—her *daed* abandoned her. That *maedel* practically had to raise herself because her brute of a *daed* was too consumed with the bottle to care for his *dochder*. By the time she turned eighteen, Abe's drinking had gotten so bad sometimes he'd pass out on their front lawn. She was probably so tired of taking care of him she did the only thing she could think to do—she took care of herself by leaving."

Seth opened his mouth to say that's not how Abe seemed to him, but Martha continued lecturing him. "You didn't know him before he gave up the booze. But I did. And I know Trina wouldn't have any part in supporting a liquor store."

Seth felt terrible. He hadn't realized Trina's grandfather had been an alcoholic, or that he'd been negligent in caring for Trina's mother. He was wrong for judging Patience. And he hoped he was wrong in imagining Trina would sell out, too.

Chapter Five

In the week following Martha's confiding in her about Freeman, Trina tried to drop hints to Timothy and Tanner about the fact she wouldn't be with them very long. She agreed with Seth it might be painful for them when she left, so she wanted to prepare them for her eventual departure. On Wednesday afternoon, as she put them down for their naps, Timothy asked if she'd still be there when he woke up.

"Of course I will," she told him, realizing she may have overdone it in warning them she wasn't going to be with them permanently. "I'm not leaving until May. I'll show you how many days that is on the calendar when you're done napping."

"Will you *kumme* to visit us after you leave?" Timothy asked.

"Well, Philadelphia is pretty far away."

"That's okay. *Englischers* can drive a car or fly in an airplane." Tanner yawned before adding, "*Daed* said he doesn't want you to sell your house."

Trina's ear perked up. "When did he say that?"

"At night when I was getting a drink. He told *Groossmammi* a weasel came to your house to ask you to put a concrete jungle in your backyard. Will there be monkeys in the jungle?"

Trina was mortified. "*Neh*, your *daed* was only teasing. After all, weasels can't talk, can they?"

Tanner shook his head and Timothy asked, "Will there still be a jungle in our backyard?"

"I'm afraid not," she said. "Although that doesn't mean there won't be two of my favorite little monkeys swinging from the trees." She tickled each boy's stomach and they laughed before rolling over and falling asleep.

Later, when Seth returned home, he didn't even have time to remove his hat before Trina asked to speak with him on the porch. He looked surprised but he agreed. She was so insulted he thought she was the kind of person who'd allow her mother's property to be exploited for the sake of selling alcohol that she didn't waste time with any pleasantries.

"For your information, I'm not selling the

property to anyone who wants to use it to build a liquor store!" she said, planting her hands on her hips.

Seth removed his hat and scratched his ear as if he hadn't quite heard right. "I suppose Martha told you about our conversation?"

"*Neh*, the *buwe* did. But that hardly matters. What matters is that I'm *not* selling the house to a developer and if you have a question about something like that, you should ask me instead of spreading rumors. Especially within earshot of the *kinner*."

Seth responded defensively, "Who are you to lecture me on what I should or shouldn't do in front of my own *buwe*?"

Scowling, Trina countered, "Who do *you* think *you* are to spread false rumors about me?"

"I didn't," he said and his shoulders drooped. "At least, I didn't intend to—I didn't know the *buwe* were still awake. But I wasn't spreading a rumor. Not exactly. I was discussing my concerns with Martha, who, by the way, adamantly informed me my fears were unfounded."

Trina's cheeks were still burning. "*Jah*, and I would have informed you of the same thing if you'd only asked me first."

"I know that now." Seth lowered his voice

and compassionately explained, "My *grooss-mammi* also told me about…about your *grooss-daadi*'s drinking problem and the effect that had on your *mamm*. I had no idea. That must have been so difficult for her."

"*Jah*, it was," Trina admitted, "which is why it's so important I honor her memory by selling her childhood home to a family who will be happy together in it."

Seth's relief was evident. "I'm really glad to hear that's your intention. And I'm sorry I didn't consult with you first instead of jumping to conclusions."

"It's alright." Trina hesitated before confessing, "Martha told me about your brother's decision, too. I can see how that would influence your perspective on *Englischers*."

"I try not to let it, but I'm afraid I'm not always successful." It was too dark to see Seth's eyes, but his voice was heavy. "So *denki* for bearing with me."

Glad their argument was over, Trina jested, "Speaking of *bears*, you're going to have two very disappointed boys on your hands. After hearing your comments about the realtor, they thought they were getting an actual jungle in their backyard."

When Seth laughed, his straight, bright teeth shone in the dark. "Serves me right, I guess."

Hesitantly, Trina said, "I wouldn't think of telling you what to do with your *buwe*, but could I offer an observation?"

"Of course."

"*Kinner* their age tend to take figurative language literally. Not only can it get their hopes up, but it can be scary for them, too. For example, the other morning I told Martha the *buwe* were so funny I almost laughed my head off. Timothy overheard and was terrified his antics were going to make my head roll off my shoulders."

"Ah, point taken," Seth said, again giving her a toothy smile.

Was he laughing at her or at the boys? "What's that smile about?" she asked.

"Oh, I was just thinking you must be a *wunderbaar* teacher. Not only because of the way you teach Timothy and Tanner, but because of the way you just made your point with me, too."

Trina's insides felt wiggly. She loved being a teacher and she was glad it showed. "*Denki*. And since you mentioned careers, I'd like to say I could see from the detail you put into your leatherwork that you care very much about their quality."

Seth adjusted his hat. "*Denki*. Did the *buwe* show you one of my harnesses in the stable?"

"*Neh.* I peeked into your shop window when I walked home from church the other day. I'd love to take a closer look when the shop is open, though."

"Whoa. You walked all the way to Main Street from church and then home again?"

"*Jah.* I'm heartier than I look."

Was she imagining it or did Seth just give her the once-over? "Some off Sunday when we're not at church, I could pick you up and take you to my shop," he suggested. "With the *buwe* and Martha, of course."

Of course—Trina understood the rules of propriety. "I'd like that. And I'd also like it if you'd check out the rest of my house for mice. The one in the cupboard is gone but I heard something scratching last night. It might have been a branch against the walls but just in case…"

"I thought you said you were hearty," Seth joked. "What harm is a little mouse going to do to you?"

Trina didn't know if she should confide in him, but since he'd been so understanding about her *mamm* and about Abe's alcoholism, she decided to risk it. "I know it's a ridiculous fear. But when you've lived in the city, or when you've been poor, it's not always mice you hear. Sometimes it's…rats." Even the word made her shudder, or maybe it was the fact she'd just confided to Seth that she and her mother had once been very poor. Suddenly self-conscious, she turned her head even though it was too dark for Seth to see her expression.

Seth cleared his throat. "I'd be happy to help rid your house of the little critters," he said warmly. "And if I'm not successful, I know two little *buwe* who act like very convincing *katze*."

They both laughed. Trina was glad what started out as an uncomfortable, intense conversation had ended so well and even gladder Seth had complimented her abilities as a teacher.

On Thursday evening after putting the boys to bed early, Seth visited Belinda Imhoff to discuss potentially courting a different woman. He would have waited to see Belinda after work on Saturday, but he had reserved that afternoon to more thoroughly mouse-proof Trina's house. He was so relieved she didn't intend to sell the property to a land developer that he would have done almost anything to get the house into better shape for a family to move into.

Belinda suggested matching him with Emma

Lamp, who was from Willow Creek. Seth had never considered courting her previously because she was so young—perhaps only eighteen or nineteen. It seemed she would have had plenty of opportunities for courtships through attending singings or other social events with youth her own age. But he wanted to keep an open mind, especially since Belinda seemed disappointed he had already decided against Fannie. Belinda suggested he try meeting her a few more times, but Seth had a sure sense that Fannie and her daughters weren't compatible with him and his family. More time wasn't going to change his mind, and he had to make the most of the next several weeks while Trina was still there to watch the boys. So, he asked Belinda to arrange for him to take Emma to his home after church that Sunday.

Because there was a torrential downpour on Saturday afternoon, he didn't allow the boys to accompany him to Trina's house while he repaired the woodwork. He didn't want them dirtying her floors as well as theirs, and Martha said she could handle them for an hour or so.

After pointing out where she'd heard the scratching sounds in the parlor, Trina retreated to the kitchen, and Seth examined the baseboards and flooring, which were definitely in need of repair. He wanted to fix them for her, as well as for any potential buyers. He was kneeling behind the sofa examining the baseboard when he heard Trina enter the room. Rising to face her, he knocked his shoulder against the end table and toppled its contents— a Bible and a framed photo—onto the floor. He managed to catch the Bible but the picture frame went crashing down and broke into several pieces that skittered across the floor.

Trina gasped. "Oh, *neh*!"

Seth clumsily stood up. "Ach, I'm sorry. I'll clean that up," he offered.

Trina dropped to her knees and picked up the broken frame, which appeared to be made out of fragments of glass. She rocked it in her arms and cried as if it were her baby that had fallen. He began collecting pieces of glass from the floor but she snapped, "Leave them alone—and leave me alone, too. I want you to go home."

"What?" Seth didn't understand why she was acting so devastated over a few pieces of glass. Even Timothy and Tanner wouldn't have cried like that over a broken object.

Her lip was quivering as she raised her tear streaked face and repeated, "Please leave."

"What about the cracks in the walls?"

"I don't care about the stupid walls or this stupid house," she wailed.

"That makes no sense," he pointed out. "You're bawling over something that's already broken instead of prioritizing something that can still be fixed."

Trina rose to her feet and held up the jagged frame. "This was important to me," she cried. "It was the most important possession I owned."

"But that's just it, it's only a possession. It's not as if it's a life that's lost." He didn't know why, but that really set Trina to sobbing. He didn't give in. "I don't understand why the *Englisch* are so preoccupied with photos anyway. It's *narrish*."

"I wouldn't expect you to understand," she wept. "Amish men don't have feelings. Or at least they don't show them if they do. They're heartless, absolutely heartless."

Heartless? That was the most preposterous thing he'd ever heard. "Oh, we have feelings, alright. But only for things that matter. We're not like the *Englisch* who care about their material possessions more than anything."

"You have no idea what we care about," Trina countered. "How could you? You're too busy judging us to understand us."

"And the *Englisch* are just plain too busy,"

Seth retorted. "Everything is hurry, hurry, hurry, now, now, now. You're pushy and impatient and overbearing."

"Oh, *denki* very much for that. Is there anything else you want to say about the *Englisch* before you leave?" Trina sniped.

Seth knew the argument had gotten out of hand, but he really resented being called heartless. "*Jah*, the *Englisch* are so concerned with being thin they don't care if they look sickly. I have healthier looking scarecrows in my garden."

He knew he'd gone too far even before Trina's expression wilted and she turned her back to him, but at that moment, he felt his remarks were justified. After all, she'd asked him what he thought of *Englischers*.

Hours later, he was still stoking the ashes of his anger, when Timothy asked, "Can we invite Trina to supper tomorrow night, *Daed*?"

"Neh," he barked and Martha popped her head up from where she was crocheting on the sofa. She always said when you crocheted for as many years as she did, you didn't need vision; you could do it in your sleep.

"Tomorrow Emma Lamp is visiting for supper," he explained, as if that were the only reason he didn't want Trina around.

"Emma Lamp?" Martha echoed. "Isn't she a little young?"

"It's not age that matters. It's maturity," Seth groused, thinking of Trina's tantrum over a broken picture frame. He didn't need a lecture from Martha but he knew one was coming when she sent the boys to the basement to ride their bikes.

"You've been moping all afternoon. Do you want to tell me what's wrong?"

"Neh," Seth replied curtly.

"Well, tell me anyway," Martha said, and as usual he gave in, explaining what had happened between him and Trina at her house.

"Can you believe it?" he asked. "I was there as a favor and she showed me no gratitude. It wasn't as if I broke her frame on purpose. And I said I was sorry!"

"What was in the picture frame?"

"A picture, of course," Seth sputtered in exasperation.

"A picture of what?"

"I don't know. I think it was of Trina and her *mamm*."

Martha nodded, but remained silent as the realization washed over Seth. He reluctantly conceded, "Alright, I suppose she valued the frame because of the photo."

"I think she valued both the photo and the frame because of the memory they contained."

Seth sighed heavily. He remembered, as irrational as it was, after Eleanor died he'd kept her prayer *kapp* hanging on the bedpost until the day he and the baby boys moved out of the house. It wasn't the *kapp* he cherished; it was that the *kapp* reminded him of all the times his wife faithfully prayed for their family.

"I'm not heartless," he muttered.

"*Neh*, you're definitely not. And Trina knows that. But in the moment, you probably seemed that way to her."

Seth went to bed that night feeling sadder than he'd felt in a long time. So much for loving his neighbor; he'd all but stomped on Trina's memories and then called her a scarecrow. He'd have to find a way to apologize.

Trina lay in bed and imagined calling a cab and running away from Willow Creek in the middle of the night without telling anyone she was going. Her mother had done it with even less education and resources than Trina had, so why couldn't she?

Her mother. The tears hadn't stopped flowing since her photo frame shattered across the floor. It was as if her mother herself was warning her about Amish men. Ha! What a joke it was for Seth to caution his sons not to get too close to her—the reverse was actually true. Trina should have been more cautious about getting too close to Seth. She had come dangerously close to trusting him, the way her mother must have trusted Trina's father at first.

"Your *daed* was the opposite of mine," Patience told Trina once she was old enough to begin dating. "He was physically and emotionally demonstrative and I was starving for affection. But that wasn't a good enough reason to marry him. When you date, Trina, don't do it out of a sense of loneliness."

Of course, Trina wasn't *dating* Seth. Not even close. But if she was honest, she had to admit she had feelings for him that were more than just neighborly congeniality. And it was largely because she was lonely. *How pathetic!* she scolded herself. She would have left Willow Creek right then, but out of spite and the sheer willfulness to prove she could make it in that community she decided she'd stay. She wasn't going to give up her inheritance—her mother's home—just because of a couple of coldhearted men like Abe and Seth.

Plus, no matter that the boys were related to Seth, she couldn't take off without at least saying goodbye to Timothy and Tanner. Nor could she leave Martha alone to care for them.

Not yet. But the instant her sixty days were up, she was out of there. She wasn't going to stick around until the house sold, either. She was feeling stronger now. She could get a teaching job again. She'd take out a loan until the sale went through so she could afford rent, or else she'd sell the house dirt cheap to the first buyer. But she wasn't going to give up what was hers simply because a clumsy ox of a man thought she was materialistic and as scrawny as a scarecrow.

The next morning when she tried to button her skirt for church, she actually had to suck in her stomach to get it to close. It was true she'd lost a lot of weight and she supposed she did look scraggy to Seth, but she was making progress. She pulled on a dress, instead, and arranged her hair in a bun at the nape of her neck instead of her usual ponytail and set off for church.

The sermon was on God's forgiveness and the pastor had hardly uttered three sentences before she realized she couldn't carry her grudge against Seth. She had to forgive him but that didn't mean everything would be the same between them again. She couldn't risk letting her defenses down a second time.

"Hi, Trina," someone said after the closing song, tapping her on the shoulder.

She turned to find Ethan giving her an enormous grin. "Hi, Ethan. It's nice to see you."

"You, too. I almost didn't recognize you with your hair like that. Are you going somewhere special?"

"Neh," she said and then repeated, "No. I'm not going anywhere special."

"Good. Then you'll let me give you a ride home?"

After confirming she didn't have special plans, Trina had no choice but to accept Ethan's offer. "Thank you. That would be nice," she agreed.

On the way they chatted about what brought them to Willow Creek. "My grandparents were Mennonites, so I've always had an interest in Mennonite and Amish culture and beliefs," Ethan explained. "I knew this is where I wanted to practice medicine. I mostly see patients in Willow Creek and one day a week I volunteer at the Highland Springs clinic for the Amish. How about you? Why did you relocate to Willow Creek?"

"I didn't," Trina said. "I mean, I'm only staying here for a couple of months because—oh, it's a long story, but I have to live here for sixty days before I can inherit the house my mother grew up in. She was Amish. Anyway, once my time is up, I'm selling the house and moving back to Philly."

"I just left Philly!" Ethan exclaimed. "That's where my fiancée lives. She'll be joining me after our wedding in June. It's a great city, but I prefer the country life here, don't you?"

"I'm becoming accustomed to it," Trina admitted, relieved to hear Ethan was engaged. So, his interest in her was merely because she was a new resident like he was, and nothing more. "I especially enjoy walking by the creek, knowing it's where my mother once walked."

"Can you believe I've been in Willow Creek for over two months and I still haven't seen the creek the town is named after?"

Trina impulsively suggested, "Oh, you'll have to take a look, then. It runs behind the property near my house."

As they were strolling by the banks of the creek a few minutes later, Trina heard a sound. "I recognize those voices," she said.

"Voices? I only heard something growl."

Trina laughed. "It's the two boys I care for during the day. They like to pretend they're animals. If I'm not mistaken, they're being bears again."

Just then, Tanner and Timothy pounced out at Trina and Ethan from behind a rock. "Rr-roar!" they thundered.

"Look, it's a pair of grizzlies!" Ethan declared good-naturedly.

"Guder nammidaag, buwe," Trina greeted them. "Stand up on your hind legs now. I want to introduce you to my friend, Ethan Gray. He's a doctor, so you might go to his office one day when you're sick and he'll make you feel better."

"Animals don't go to doctors. They go to vegetarians," Timothy said wisely, cracking Ethan up. After they told Ethan their names, Trina asked them if they were walking with Martha.

"Neh. We're with *Daed* and Emma," Timothy answered.

Trina's stomach did a flip and she suddenly felt dejected. But after what she'd learned yesterday about Seth's feelings—or lack of feelings—toward her, why should she care if she bumped into him and some new woman he was apparently courting?

"Timothy, Tanner!" Seth's voice cut through the crisp air. "Where are you?"

"We're here with Trina," Tanner bellowed back.

"What have I told you about staying within my sight near the creek?" Seth asked the boys before greeting Trina or Ethan. "If you wander off again, we'll have to march right back to the house and you won't be able to return for an entire week."

"Sorry, *Daed*." The boys hung their heads.

"Oh, look, it's Dr. Gray," a young woman said when she caught up with Seth. She had light blond hair and a sturdy, feminine shape. Her skin was so pink and her face so full it looked like she literally had apples in her cheeks. No doubt she was just the kind of healthy, patient, sensible woman Seth was looking for.

"Emma... Lamp, isn't it?" Ethan asked.

"*Jah*. What a *gut* memory." Emma even had dimples when she smiled. She was the picture of Amish benevolence. "Seth Helmuth, have you met Dr. Gray? He took care of my brother when he came down with a nasty flu."

"Please, call me Ethan." The doctor smiled. Trina noticed Ethan didn't extend his hand to shake; apparently, he knew the customs already. To Emma he said, "How is Thomas doing?"

"He's better than ever before. Tormenting our sisters and chasing them around the barn."

"Glad to hear it. I assume you know Trina Smith?" Ethan asked, gesturing toward her.

"Only by reputation," Emma said, smiling. "The moment I walked through the door, the *buwe* showed me games you taught them. They're very fond of you."

Oh, no. Emma was nice as well as sweet and pretty. "I'm fond of them, too," Trina said. She could hardly look in Seth's direction, lest she see *his* fondness for Emma in his eyes. Or worse, his disdain for Trina.

"Looks like we're going in opposite directions, so we'll keep walking," Seth said. "Now, where did those two scamper off to?"

"I believe they're in the den to our right, up ahead," Emma said, motioning toward a large rock the boys had covered with sticks and fern. Trina had to give it to her, she was playing along with their games well. As if reading Trina's thoughts, Emma winked at her and said, "I've got a brother and two little sisters around their age at home."

Wow, she must have been really young herself to have siblings that age! Trina felt glum all the way back to the house so she was happy when Ethan accepted her invitation for tea and dessert. At least he seemed to like her. Granted, he appeared to like her the way a big brother would, which made her feel embarrassed she'd ever suspected him of being interested in dating her.

"I don't know, Trina," he said slowly before

leaving. "Willow Creek is awfully beautiful. Are you sure you want to leave it behind for Philly?"

"I'm sure," she said.

On the way home from dropping off Emma, Seth felt sick to his stomach and his palms were sweaty. It wasn't nervousness. Not about Emma, anyway. No, it was easy to be around her. She was pleasant, lighthearted and she got along well with the boys. But she was also young. Too young. It wasn't that she was immature, exactly, but in a way her youthful innocence made Seth feel as if he had another child in his care. Halfway through the afternoon he decided to tell Belinda Imhoff he'd made a mistake and he'd give a courtship with Fannie Jantzi one more try.

But for now, he had to apologize to Trina and it was unnerving him like nothing ever had before. Bumping into her in the woods had been uncomfortable and he wished he hadn't seen her with Ethan. An *Englisch* pediatrician. Who could be better for Trina? Together they'd make the perfect couple, with her teaching children and him healing them. Seth should have been happy that she'd found a friend in Willow Creek. A boyfriend, even—

someone who might be a good match. But he wasn't happy. And the fact he wasn't happy was unsettling. Furthermore, he was doubly upset because he had to apologize to her and he didn't know if she'd accept his apology.

She'd hardly glanced his way in the woods, although for his part he'd noticed she wore her hair in a neat bun. With her face framed by its softness, her cheekbones looked less severe and her eyes stood out even more. Seth shook his head. How could he have been so boorish as to imply she looked like a scarecrow? He'd never found any *Englischer* so attractive before. Not simply because of her eyes and height and the way she carried herself, but because of the way her character manifested itself through her physical traits. It pained him to think she thought of him as heartless.

He took extra care stabling his horse, procrastinating before he crossed the yard to Trina's house. Instead of inviting him in when he asked to speak to her, she stepped onto the porch, closing the door behind her. She wasn't wearing a coat; he'd have to make this quick.

"I've *kumme* to apologize. I'm truly sorry for breaking your picture frame," he began. "But I'm even sorrier for hurting you. I shouldn't have implied you're overly concerned with possessions. Later, when I thought things over,

I realized I just said that because I... I was trying to do something helpful for you and instead I broke your frame. I felt like such a klutz that I somehow turned things around and tried to pin the blame on you for valuing a possession instead of acknowledging I'd ruined something that was special to you."

Trina didn't say anything until she'd walked past him and stood by the railing of the porch, gazing at the sky. "I don't own many material things, but the picture frame was a gift from my *mamm*."

Seth was quiet, sensing he needed to give her time to say her piece before she forgave him.

"She gave it to me the Christmas before she became ill. She'd bought it at the Cape—Cape Cod, in Massachusetts. I don't know how she could have afforded it, but—" Trina choked and a sob escaped her lips.

Seth walked to her, removed his coat and draped it around her shoulders. "What is one of your favorite memories of being at Cape Cod with your mother?" he asked.

Trina sniffed and gestured out toward the lawn, as if remembering the ocean. "We loved to get up early in the morning and go to the beach before anyone else arrived. There were these little tiny birds called sandpipers that ran along the edge of the surf. They were so quick they made us laugh." Trina wiped her eyes with the back of her hand and added wryly, "You wouldn't like them, they looked like they were in a hurry."

Seth chortled. "I'm sorry for saying that, too. I know not all *Englischers* are in a hurry."

"Most of them are. I don't disagree with you on that," Trina said. "But I'm not."

"And I'm not heartless," Seth said, quietly but firmly. "But I understand that your *groossdaadi* acted that way to your *mamm*."

"Oh, Seth!" Trina exclaimed, angling sideways to look at him again. "I'm so sorry I said that. You have a bigger heart than any man I know. The amount of love and care you show for Timothy and Tanner—and for Martha, too—well, I've never seen a man demonstrate anything like it."

From the way his heart was battering his ribs, Seth was sure Trina could hear it. He replied, "And I'm sorry for implying you look like a scarecrow."

"Well, I have lost a lot of weight this past year and those *seh* of yours can make me look pretty disheveled by the end of the day."

Neh. You're the best sight I see at the end of my day, Seth thought. It was a bold sentiment and he was in a dangerous position to think such a thing, much less to say it. He didn't, of course, but neither did he stop looking at her. There was something about her lips that made them seem as irresistible as the taste of funny cake. Yet he had to resist. She was an *Englischer*, like Freeman's wife. In a throaty voice he said, "*Jah,* my sons can have that effect on a person. But you don't look disheveled now. I like your hair like that."

"*Denki.*" Trina lifted her hand to the nape of her neck and turned back toward the lawn in one graceful motion. She paused before playfully referencing her angry remark from the previous day, "Anyway, if you're willing, I'd still like you to fix my stupid walls."

"*Jah*, I'm still willing to fix the stupid walls in your stupid house," he said and they both laughed.

But he wasn't laughing later that night in bed. He was agonizing over how much he had longed to kiss an *Englischer*. It was forbidden by the *Ordnung*, but even if it weren't, it was forbidden by him, personally. His family had already paid dearly for allowing one *Englischer* into their lives, and Kristine had claimed she was going to become Amish. Trina made no such promise; on the contrary, she was leaving in a matter of weeks.

If only Seth had been ashamed and regretful that he wanted to kiss her, he could confess and be done with it. But the sorry truth was, he may have been ashamed of it, but he still wished to kiss Trina.

That's lecherich, he thought. *I'd never do such a thing. Never!*

Besides, for all he could guess, Trina was interested in Ethan. Seth knew the best way to rid his mind of fanciful thoughts about her was to keep squarely focused on courting an Amish woman, and before falling asleep he decided he'd definitely invite Fannie and her daughters to the house for supper at the first opportunity.

Chapter Six

As pleased as Trina was that she and Seth had cleared the air, she was unnerved by what had transpired—or nearly transpired—between them. It was one thing for him to give her his coat; that was a gallant gesture, but one he would have made to Martha, as well as to any woman who was cold. But the way he'd looked at her before he told her he liked her hair... She wasn't misinterpreting the ardor of his expression, was she? *Don't be silly,* she told herself. *I was wrong about Ethan's intentions and I'm probably wrong about Seth's, too.*

Not that it mattered much. She was *Englisch* and he was Amish, so there was no possibility of any romantic relationship between them. She didn't want one, either. Alright, perhaps she wanted one a little. Perhaps she wanted him to kiss her instead of just look like he wanted to kiss her. But that was inconceivable. It was permissible to be friends with him and to care for his children, but after all Patience had gone through to raise her daughter as an *Englischer*, Trina felt disloyal to her *mamm*'s memory for even entertaining thoughts of kissing an Amish man. Besides, Seth was courting Emma. That was serious; that was for the explicit purpose of pursuing a marriage relationship. It wasn't just some passing infatuation.

Trina knew what she needed to do was to call a few realtors and start preparing to sell the house. She couldn't officially put it on the market until May, but she decided she should probably get the ball rolling. The sooner it sold, the sooner she could go back to Philly. The summer months were always the best hiring times for new teachers, so she didn't want to miss those opportunities.

For the rest of the week, Trina wore her hair up in a ponytail again because she felt too self-conscious to be reminded of Seth's compliment. She went out of her way to focus their discussions on the boys whenever she was with Seth, and if she wasn't mistaken, he also seemed to limit their conversations to the weather or his sons. And on Saturday evening, when they all traveled to the *Englisch* store in Highland Springs, Trina sat in the back with the boys on the way there. On the way back, however, Martha insisted she take the front seat next to Seth.

Trina kept her arm tight to her side so she wouldn't inadvertently bump into him as the buggy wiggled toward home. They were quiet for a while as Martha and the boys chatted in the back until the silence between them felt unnatural.

"It's getting warmer. I hardly need this blanket any longer." Trina referenced the wool blanket on her lap, at a loss for what else to discuss.

"Oh, here, I can put it in the back for you if you're too hot," Seth replied.

His hand grazed Trina's knee as he reached for it. At the same time, Trina tried to grab it, saying, "*Neh*, that's okay. I just meant the weather is changing." Their hands collided on her lap and they both immediately pulled back. Trina's arm buzzed as if she'd touched an electric fence.

"*Jah*, spring will be here soon," Seth blandly remarked. "I mean, I know it's here on the calendar, but it will be here in the weather, too."

Trina giggled nervously. This conversation was becoming more ridiculous by the sentence. "I'm almost to the end of my fourth week here. Do you know anyone who wants to buy a house?" she joked nervously.

"I wish I did." Seth's comment disappointed Trina. Was she expecting him to say he was sorry to see her go—if not for his sake, then for the boys'? He continued, "That way I'd know who our neighbors were before they moved in."

"Isn't part of being neighborly taking time to get to know the people living next door?" Trina wondered aloud. As soon as she asked the question she worried if it sounded flirtatious, which wasn't her intention.

"*Jah,* I suppose you're right," Seth allowed. "I only meant I'd like to know in general if they're *Englisch* or Amish so I could put up a fence ahead of time if necessary."

Now Trina was annoyed. "Don't tell me, the fence would keep the *Englisch* out of your yard." *And out of your life,* she thought. "Has having me for a neighbor been that bad?"

Although he kept his eyes on the road, Seth emphatically shook his head. "*Neh*, I didn't mean it like that. I'd want to build a fence to keep the *kinner* in. If the neighbors are *Englisch* and they have cars, I don't want the *kinner* running over there."

Relaxing, Trina said, "The *buwe* are usually pretty *gut* about not going where they shouldn't—unless they're pretending to be wild creatures down by the creek."

"It's not Timothy and Tanner I'm worried about. It's Fannie's girls. They don't seem to mind too well."

Trina was too surprised to hold her tongue. "Fannie's girls? What about Emma?" she asked. "I thought you were courting Emma."

"Emma's too young. Barely twenty," Seth said.

So that was it, then? Emma didn't work out so he simply defaulted to the better of his two choices and now he was already considering marriage with Fannie? "Wow. And you think *Englischers* are impatient," she couldn't help saying snidely under her breath.

"What?"

Quietly so no one else would hear, and staring straight ahead, Trina said, "You've been on what, two dates with Fannie and you're already considering building a fence for her *kinner*? That must mean you plan to marry her. Even the *Englisch* don't rush into marriage that quickly."

Seth huffed so loudly Trina thought it was the horse at first. "I've told you, we don't call it *dating*. But when you've been married before you know what you're looking for in a spouse."

"It may be true that you know what qualities you're looking for in a woman, but finding them doesn't necessarily mean you've found love, does it?" Trina understood she was crossing a line by talking about such things with an Amish man but she felt too argumentative to give in.

"The Amish tend to base our decisions on practical considerations, not emotional ones. Love is a choice. It's something you work at developing. It's not something that you either have or don't have."

"So you'd marry a woman you're not in love with?"

"Not that I think it's appropriate to be having this conversation, but *jah*, I'd marry a woman I wasn't necessarily 'in love with.' Because being 'in love' is just an emotion and emotions are fickle. They're dangerous," Seth explained. He added, "Over time and with work and mutual cooperation, a couple can *kumme* to love each other deeply."

Trina didn't know how to respond to that. She didn't necessarily disagree with Seth, but she certainly didn't agree fully, either. After all, her mother had fallen in love with her father based on her feelings, and look where that had gotten her. Conversely, her mother's father had shown a severe lack of emotion and that was damaging, too.

Trina swallowed and forced herself to say, "Well, then, I'm glad for you if you've found what you're looking for in a spouse. As soon as I know whether the people who buy the house are *Englisch* or Amish, I'll be sure to tell you."

Seth couldn't believe he'd just indicated to Trina he intended to marry Fannie. He felt as verbally awkward as he was physically, touching her knee, bumping her hand; it had thrown him off. Especially since all week he'd tried to restrict his contact and dull his conversations with her. Now she was sitting right next to him, talking about one of the most intimate subjects they could discuss. As much as he denied the power of emotions, his were wreaking havoc on him. He feared he'd come across as even more of a dope if he tried to explain.

The truth was, he wasn't actually *planning* to make a fence for Fannie's daughters— he'd just been thinking aloud. In his mind, it was more like a complaint, as in, "*If* I were to marry Fannie, I'd better put a fence up because her girls are ill behaved." The emphasis had been on the girls' behavior, not on marriage, but how would Trina have known that? He was relieved he wouldn't have to see her the following day. Maybe by Monday some of his embarrassment would have burned off and he wouldn't feel so oafish around her again.

After the next morning's worship, Timothy excitedly asked, "Can we *kumme* with you to get Fannie and her *dechder*, *Daed*?"

Seth didn't think it was a good idea to have the children's initial introduction to each other taking place within the confines of a crowded buggy. "*Neh*, but as soon as Hope and Greta arrive, we'll all take a walk along the creek together. For now I want you to stay here and help *Groossmammi* with whatever she needs."

"What I need is for Trina to *kumme* and help me put together a light supper," Martha grumbled.

"*Neh!*" Seth objected. He couldn't think of anything worse than having Trina around after their conversation yesterday. She'd no doubt scrutinize every interaction between him and Fannie and see there was no spark—no *emotional* connection—between them. "Trina is probably still at her church. Besides, Fannie will help you with whatever you need to do in the kitchen."

"That's what I'm afraid of," Martha muttered.

Her comment made Seth wonder why he was going through with introducing Fannie's children to his. He didn't want to make his household problems worse by bringing in disobedient children and a pushy woman who clashed with Martha. But as he was pulling out of their lane onto the main road, he saw a car turning onto Trina's lane: Ethan was giving Trina a ride home. Again. Seth could guess what this meant; they were falling in love. It served as a reminder to Seth to stay focused on following through with his own plans for matrimony.

The girls sang all the way back to his house and Fannie sang with them. While he appreciated their desire to praise the Lord with songs on the Sabbath, Seth felt like Fannie was so involved in amusing her children she had no time to speak with him, and his thoughts again wandered to Trina. Her speaking voice was so euphonious he wondered what she sounded like singing. Once, before entering the house, he'd heard her warbling through the door as she was washing dishes, but as soon as he turned the knob, she stopped... A dip in the road jarred the buggy and Seth realized he shouldn't be thinking of Trina, especially while he was courting Fannie, so he joined the others in song until they arrived at his house.

Martha must have told the boys they could wait outside as long as they didn't leave the porch, because they were both hopping up and down on the stairs without venturing into the yard when the buggy pulled up.

"Do you want to see the dens we built by the creek?" Tanner asked as soon as he and Timothy had been introduced to Hope and Greta.

"How about if we go inside first?" Fannie suggested. "The girls want to meet your *groossmammi* and I'm sure she's prepared us something to eat. We don't want it to get cold."

Seth thought it was presumptuous of Fannie to think there was a hot meal waiting. Firstly, he hoped Martha hadn't used the oven or stove, no matter how competent she said she was around it. Secondly, on the Sabbath most of Willow Creek's Amish had cold cuts and fruit or molasses and peanut butter on bread, not a warm meal. But Seth had warned the boys they needed to be polite to their guests and he was pleased when they agreed with Fannie. They even allowed the girls to enter the house first.

"Wilkom," Martha said in their general direction. She was standing at the sink, drying her hands on a towel. She bent down toward Greta and said, "I'm Martha and you must be Greta." Standing a little straighter so her head was even with Hope's, she added, "Which means you're Hope, right?"

"How did she know that?" Hope asked her

mother, as if Martha couldn't hear. "You said she was blind."

Seth cringed but his grandmother, who was being as polite as he'd warned the boys they had to be, just chuckled and said, "People sometimes say bats are blind, too, but have you ever seen one fly into a wall?"

Hope shook her head. *"Neh."*

Timothy told her, "That's because they have something called echo…um, echo…"

Seth helped him out. "Echolocation."

"Echolocation," Timothy repeated. "Trina read it to us in a book Ruth Graber brought from the library."

"You have echo—the thing he said?" Hope asked Martha incredulously.

Tanner answered before Martha could. *"Neh.* Only bats have that. But my *groossmammi* has eyes in the back of her head even if the eyes in front of her head are blurry. So if you do something disobedient behind her, she'll catch you."

Seth, Martha and Fannie all laughed heartily. Martha must have used that expression in front of the boys. Trina was right; they seemed to take everything literally. But once again, Seth had to banish thoughts of her.

The seven of them sat down for dinner and Seth was relieved to see that today the girls' table manners were about as good as his boys', even though Greta spilled a glass of milk in a way Seth suspected was deliberate.

"I'm sorry. This happens daily," Fannie said. "She's at that age, you know, where her fingers are still too small to grasp a glass in one hand, but she forgets to use both hands. It's probably like that with Timothy and Tanner, too."

Although his grandmother couldn't have seen the way Greta tipped her glass over, Seth suspected if it had been Timothy or Tanner, Martha would have told them an accident that happened every day wasn't an accident. Instead, she simply said, "No sense crying over spilled milk," and asked Seth to refill Greta's glass for her.

"But I don't want more milk," Greta whined when he set it in front of her.

"I'll drink it," Fannie quickly offered. "It will taste *gut* with dessert."

Now Seth was perturbed. Didn't Fannie ever wait until she was offered? "I'm not certain *Groossmammi* had an opportunity to make dessert yesterday, since we didn't get to the market until later last night—"

"You're right. I didn't. I know it's the Sabbath, but I don't think there's any harm in my whipping up a batch of cookies in the oven while you're taking a walk. It's a way to show hospitality and the Lord loves it when we reflect His character like that," Martha rationalized.

As the others were donning their coats and shawls, Seth whispered to Martha, "You don't have to make dessert, *Groossmammi*. Really. We've had plenty to eat."

"You just don't want me starting another fire."

She was right; her safety was part of Seth's concern. But he was also annoyed Fannie was putting Martha in a position of feeling she wasn't being hospitable. What did the woman expect from his eighty-three-year-old grandmother?

Martha continued, "I'll be fine. Just turn the oven on 375 for me before you go. By the time you return, I'll be done and you can check to make sure it's off. Nothing is on the stovetop so there's no chance of anything catching fire."

Seth wanted to protest but he knew that would be adding insult to injury. Especially if Fannie became worried, too, and offered to stay behind and help Martha bake.

"Denki, Groossmammi," he whispered, kissing her on top of her prayer *kapp* before heading to the creek with the others.

Trina spread herself across a big rock alongside the creek. Her mother had referred to the boulder as Bed Rock, which was a play on words and also a descriptive phrase because the large rock's surface was as flat as a bed. The day was unseasonably warm and Trina positioned her face to the sun to absorb its warmth. But her head was thrumming so she sat up again and loosened her hair from its elastic band. Then she removed her jacket, rolled it into a pillow and lay back against it. That was better.

She was out of sorts and she didn't know why. That morning in church, she'd asked Sherman and Mabel if they knew a reputable realtor in the area and they recommended someone in the congregation. That person was out of town, but Mabel promised to introduce Trina to her as soon as the realtor returned.

This should have made Trina happy, but instead she was downcast. She didn't like to think about leaving Willow Creek. Her mother was in Heaven; of that she was sure. But there was something about being in the town where Patience had lived as a girl that made Trina feel closer to her. Not all of the memories of her mother's childhood there were pleasant, but many of them—especially those that didn't involve her father—were, and it brought Trina joy to see the places or meet the people her mother once knew.

Plus, Trina was growing terribly fond of the boys. Instead of reminding them she'd be leaving soon, she should have worked harder at reminding herself. *Maybe the house won't sell right away and I can watch them until school lets out in June*, she thought. But then what? Wasn't she postponing the inevitable? What did she hope to gain by staying longer in Willow Creek?

She knew the answer: she wanted more time with Seth. She felt like a traitor to her mother to even think the thought, but she couldn't help it. She liked him in a way she hadn't liked any man before. It was partly because he was so loving toward his family and partly because he'd been protective and understanding of her.

It was also because of his dependability and loyalty. With all of the other important males in her life, once times got tough, the men got lost. Her grandfather emotionally abandoned her mother when he lost his wife. Her father took off when he was confronted with the responsibilities of parenthood. Her boyfriend dumped Trina when her mother was ill. Seth had lost his wife and mother and brother, but he stayed true to his faith and to his boys and grandmother. In a way, he'd stayed true to Trina, too, by making up instead of firing her after they'd had an argument. No man had ever apologized like that for hurting her before.

Granted, theirs was a small argument. And she was his employee, so it was in his best interest to reconcile. So she feared she was kidding herself to believe he felt the same strong pull toward her that she felt toward him. And even if he did, there was no chance he'd ever act on those feelings. There was no chance he'd *date* her; the very term was too *Englisch* for his liking.

What if I were to become Amish? The thought whisked over her like a warm breeze rattling a few branches overhead. No, Trina could no sooner convert than Seth could become *Englisch*. If Patience Kauffman had wanted her daughter to be Amish, she would have returned to her community after Richard Smith divorced her. But Trina's mother wanted the exact opposite. She chose poverty and isolation instead of bringing Trina up in an Amish community, so there was no way Trina was going to convert just to capture the attention of an Amish man.

An Amish man, who, at that very moment, was courting someone he intended to wed. *Don't lose sight of that*, she told herself. Yet no matter how illogical it was, her emotions said otherwise. She actually felt sick with longing for Seth. Maybe he was right—maybe emotions were dangerous. She opened her eyes but the sun made her see blinking spots so she closed them again.

She must have dropped off to sleep because she was awakened by the voices of children. She sat up to find Timothy and Tanner clambering up the steep side of the rock.

"Hi, Trina," they chorused. "We're playing mountain lions. These are our new friends, Hope and Greta."

Trina greeted them and then as she pulled her jacket back on, she asked if they'd all wandered off by themselves.

"*Daed* said it was alright as long as we stopped at this rock," Timothy explained.

Standing below, Hope rolled her eyes and said, "I told Seth I'd keep an eye on them."

Trina didn't know whether to think the girl was funny or precocious. "I'll climb down and let you mountain lions have this rock, then," she said.

"Aww," whined Tanner. "Please don't leave. You can be the lioness of the pride."

"*Jah,*" Timothy agreed, admiringly adding, "Your hair looks like a mane."

Trina touched her head. She'd forgotten she'd loosened her hair. Where had her elastic band gone? She thought she'd set it right beside her. She didn't care. She had to get down from the rock before Fannie and Seth arrived. Not only did she not want to see Seth, but she didn't want either Seth or Fannie to see her. There was no ladylike way to descend the rock and she didn't want to appear immodest in front of Fannie. But it was too late.

"Why, look, it's the *buwe*'s nanny," Fannie said, and Trina bristled at being referred to by her occupation instead of her name.

"You may have forgotten, but her name is Trina," Seth said. Trina could have hugged him for that. "Sorry if the *kinner* interrupted your peace."

"*Daed,* we're not *kinner.* We're cubs," Tanner interjected. "And Trina's the lioness of our pride."

"Actually, I was just leaving, Tanner. I'll see you tomorrow," Trina said. She scooted on her bottom to the edge of the rock and peered over. If she jumped, she'd probably fall to her knees and hands upon landing. But if she used the same crevices to lower herself as she'd used to climb up, she'd appear unladylike. And now that she'd wiggled this far to the edge, the only way she could lower herself using the crevices was to roll onto her belly and squirm back to the other side of the rock. She dangled her legs over the side, wondering what to do.

"Here, let me give you a hand," Seth offered, stretching his arms upward.

Was he going to lift her down under her armpits like a child? She couldn't have been more embarrassed. He couldn't reach that high, so she'd have to jump into his arms. What if she knocked him over?

"You'll have to push yourself off a little to clear the edge," he said. "Don't worry, I'll catch you. It might be clumsy but I won't let you get hurt."

Trina hesitated. It might be better just to jump without his help and take her knocks.

"*Buwe*, I want you to *kumme* down, too. You don't want to get stuck like Trina did," Fannie instructed. Timothy and Tanner were the ones who'd shown Trina how to navigate the rock in the first place; they were expert climbers. Still, they obeyed Fannie without complaint.

After they scrambled down, Timothy said to the girls standing nearby, "*Kumme*, we'll show you where the elephants live in the grass by the water. They're prey for lions."

"I'll follow them while you help her," Fannie directed and the five of them disappeared into the woods.

"I really can get down by myself now," Trina told Seth. "I just didn't want everyone watching me. Please, go ahead and catch up with the others. I'll be fine."

Seth didn't seem to be in a hurry to leave. "Just jump, Trina. I'll catch you. You can trust me."

The words resonated in Trina's heart. What man could she ever really trust? "Okay," she agreed reluctantly. "One, two, three!"

She lurched forward and her hair flew out around her like a cape. Seth didn't so much catch her as ease her to the ground in a sort of awkward embrace. Right before he released her, she felt his beard softly brush her cheek.

"Ugh," Seth groaned.

"Sorry. Did I kick you?"

"*Neh*, you're just a lot heavier than you look."

"Coming from you, that's a compliment." Trina giggled.

Seth was so close she could smell the peanut butter on his breath. He lifted his hand and Trina actually thought he was going to caress her cheek but instead he picked a leaf from her hair. "You have vegetation in your mane," he gibed.

Trina giggled again. "*Denki* for helping me down. I'll stay here awhile, so you and Fannie and the *kinner* will have privacy on your outing."

As Seth opened his mouth to reply, in the distance Fannie yelled, "Seth, I can't find Tanner."

A panicked look crossed Seth's face, but Trina said, "It's alright, I know where they probably are. I'll go this way, you go check up the hill." She broke into a hard run, knowing where the boys pretended elephants lived. It was a reedy place close to the creek where it wasn't always possible to tell where the embankment ended and the water began. Trina never allowed them to go anywhere near it unless they were holding her hand.

Sprinting past Fannie, her daughters and Timothy, Trina called, "Tanner! Where are you? Say my name!"

When her command was met with silence, Trina charged into the reeds, shouting, until she reached the water's edge. Then she slogged through that, too. Her shoes and socks were wet and the hem of her skirt was weighted down with water, sticking to her legs. "Tanner! Tanner!" she shouted, feeling lightheaded. She waded deeper and deeper until she was up to her thighs in the frigid water. The current was moving at a quick clip and she struggled to remain upright.

"Trina, we found him," Seth yelled from far away. "Trina?"

Denki, she prayed. *Denki, Lord.* She splashed back toward the embankment and up the hill where the others were calling her. "Here I am," she squawked, her throat too dry for her voice to be heard.

"Trina!" Tanner called when he finally spotted her. He barreled straight for her. The force almost knocked her over as he hugged her legs. "Are you okay?"

Nearly sobbing from exertion and relief, she bent to kiss his head multiple times. "*Jah*, I'm fine. Are you okay?"

He looked up at her, tipping his head so far back she could see his nostrils. "*Jah.*"

Just then Seth clambered down the hill. "I'm so sorry about that, Trina," he said. His eyes were blazing. "Tanner was in one of their make-believe dens and he couldn't hear Fannie calling him. She was worried he fell into the creek."

"But, *Daed,* you told me I should never go near the creek by myself," Tanner said as his round eyes sprang tears. "I wouldn't disobey."

"We know you wouldn't," Trina said. "It's okay, Tanner. Everyone's okay."

Fannie came loping down the hill with her hand pressed to her mouth. "That had me so worried," she lamented.

Placing her hands on her hips, Hope told Trina, "I think you may be taking things a little too far in telling them about animals."

In all of Trina's years of teaching children,

she'd encountered some inappropriate language, but no child had ever had the nerve to admonish her as Hope was doing now. Trina kept silent so she wouldn't embarrass Seth's guests by speaking her mind, but she felt like telling the girl to show some respect or go home immediately.

"You've got to be freezing," Seth said. "Let's get you to our house. We've got a nice fire going. Martha's making cookies and she'll give you dry clothes while Fannie puts on a kettle."

"*Denki*, but I just want to go home and dry off there," Trina said. Her head was really pulsating now and her legs were tottery as she started toward her house.

"Funny, isn't it?" Fannie tittered. "Both times I've seen you so far you've been soaking wet."

That was the last thing Trina remembered before everything went dark.

Seth had been walking behind Trina and he noticed something was off about her gait and the way she was speaking, so when she staggered he was right there to keep her from falling and hitting her head. She collapsed backward into his arms and he gently lowered her to the ground. Kneeling beside her, he forcefully jiggled her arm.

"Trina, wake up. Trina, open your eyes," he said loudly. She immediately blinked and lifted her hand to rub her eyes. She couldn't have been out for more than a few seconds, but he needed to be sure she was alright. "Trina, who am I? Can you tell me my name?"

"You don't know?" she asked, a wry smile flickering across her pale face. "Seth Helmuth," she said to his satisfaction. "I'm alright. I have a *koppweh*, that's all." She groaned when she tried to sit up. This time, Seth didn't ask permission to take her home. He simply swept her up in his arms and carried her to his house, despite her protests and Fannie's pouting. He didn't set her down until he'd settled her into a rocking chair near the fire in his parlor.

"What happened?" Martha asked as she followed them from the kitchen, wringing her hands. The house smelled of cookies, not of smoke. That was at least one good thing. Seth relayed what had occurred while the children added their comments and Fannie remained silent, warming her hands by the stove as if she'd been the one who'd waded through the water to rescue Tanner.

"I'm fine," Trina said when they finished talking. "I think Seth wanted to prove to Fannie how strong he is by carrying me, that's all."

Seth knew Trina was attempting to smooth things over between him and Fannie, and he appreciated the gesture, especially considering how rude Fannie had been to her. He suggested Fannie should take the children into the kitchen to have some cookies and put on tea. Then he told his grandmother, "Trina needs something dry to wear."

"I'll say she does," Martha said, pressing her hand to Trina's forehead. "This *maedel* is cold and clammy. How long was she unconscious? We ought to take her to the doctor."

Seth was hesitant. On a Sunday, the only doctor they could take her to was in the ER at the hospital in Highland Springs. Ever since Freeman ran off with Kristine and she resumed her job as a nurse, Seth worried he might bump into one of their friends at the hospital, even though Freeman and Kristine had long since moved out of the area. Seth didn't want anyone to inquire about his brother and stir up sad memories.

"*Neh,* no doctor," Trina insisted. "I'm fine, really. I just need some sleep."

Seth was relieved but still felt concerned. "What about your friend Ethan? Can we ask him to take a look at you? I'll use the phone shanty to call him, unless you know where he lives."

"I do, but please don't bother yourself," Trina said weakly. "I've already spoiled your afternoon."

"It's not a bother. I'll stop at Ethan's on the way back from taking Fannie and her *meed* home."

"Please let him, Trina. Otherwise I'm going to worry about you all night and I won't get any sleep," Martha said. Like most people, Trina couldn't refuse the older woman's wishes, but she did insist on going home and putting her own clothes on and climbing into her own bed. Martha said she'd go with her.

After Seth escorted them to Trina's house and got the fire roaring, he took everyone, including his boys, to drop Fannie off in Elmsville. He left the boys in the buggy while he walked the others to the door. After the girls had gone inside, Fannie frankly stated, "I don't think you and I are a match, Seth."

After a startled pause, he said, "*Denki* for your honesty, Fannie. I wish you *Gott*'s best in finding a suitable spouse."

Fannie crossed her arms and furrowed her eyebrows. "Don't you even want to know why I don't think we're a match?"

Feeling as if it would be rude to say it wasn't

necessary since he had come to the same conclusion, Seth said, "Please tell me."

"I don't think we're a *gut* match because I wouldn't ever agree to be courted by a man who is inappropriately friendly with an *Englisch* woman."

He didn't know what to say. The problem was, there was nothing he *could* say. Like it or not, she was right.

Fannie waited for a second and when Seth didn't deny it, she closed the door in his face.

Chapter Seven

Martha propped the pillows up behind Trina and urged her to drink a glass of water. Then she said, "You rest. I'll be right in the parlor if you need anything."

"Please, don't go," Trina requested, so Martha sat down on the end of the bed. Trina closed her eyes. Feeling like a child, she said, "My *mamm* used to sit on the end of the bed when I was sick. I always felt comforted by the weight of her body on the mattress near my feet."

"*Jah*, she used to tuck her feet beneath me when she was sick," Martha said.

Martha had been there to comfort her mother when she was sick? Trina was glad to know that. "Sometimes I wondered how she became such a *gut mamm* since her own *mamm* died when she was so young. *Denki*, Martha, for teaching her."

"Oh, I can't take credit for that, dear. Your *groossmammi* was as loving as anyone could be. Even if Patience was too young to remember, those things still leave an impression on a *kin*."

"Mmm," Trina murmured. She felt comfortably drowsy but she didn't want Martha to stop talking to her. She forced herself to open her eyes. "Speaking of *kinner*, what did you think of Fannie's *dechder*?"

"Judging from the fact you have to ask, I probably think the same thing you think." Martha chuckled. "But Seth is determined to find a wife, so I try to keep my mouth shut and be supportive. What that young man doesn't seem to realize is it might be better if…"

Trina drifted off until two people, a man and a woman, began speaking in hushed tones at the end of her bed. She dreamed it was her father and mother. Or maybe she was remembering the Christmas her father came to visit and she'd had chicken pox. It was one of the only times she heard genuine concern in his voice as he asked her mother how she was doing…

But no, it was Ethan talking to Martha, who was recounting what happened at the creek.

"I'm not a *kin*," she said aloud, realizing she wasn't dreaming after all.

Ethan chuckled. "That's okay, just because I'm a pediatrician doesn't mean I can't determine the state of your health."

Trina tried to say that's not what she meant, but her mouth wouldn't cooperate. Martha supported Trina's head and lifted a glass of water to her lips. The room seemed to come into focus again. After taking her vital signs and asking a few questions, Ethan said he thought she might be suffering from shock. And possibly anemia, since she was so thin and pale.

"I want to take your blood and run a few tests, but you had quite a scare. You're also dehydrated, which could have given you the headache originally," he explained. "You'll need plenty of fluids and lots of rest for the next three days."

Trina smiled wanly. "I'm not sure how much rest Timothy and Tanner will let me have, but maybe if we—"

Ethan was suddenly very serious. "You won't be able to take care of Timothy and Tanner."

"But—"

"You need to take care of yourself, Trina. In fact, someone else needs to help take care of you."

"But I don't—"

"I'll contact one of the women from church. I know several people who will be happy to stay with you for a few nights."

"Nonsense!" Martha declared. "We'll take care of Trina ourselves."

Ethan seemed to sense he'd better not contradict her. He took a vial of Trina's blood and was pressing cotton against her arm when they heard footsteps on the porch, followed by a tentative knock and then Seth calling, "Hello? May we *kumme* in?"

"We're in here," Martha answered, removing her shawl and draping it modestly around Trina's shoulders.

"My hair," Trina said, suddenly self-conscious about how she looked.

"You're fine," Martha answered.

"She's fine?" Seth repeated hopefully, apparently thinking Martha was referring to Trina's condition.

"She will be, after a few days' rest," Ethan replied. "And lots of fluids."

"Oh, *gut*." Seth sighed, looking straight at Trina instead of at Ethan. She felt woozy again.

"Is Trina alright?" Tanner or Timothy piped up from the hall in squeaky voices.

"*Jah*, but she won't be if you two *buwe* don't allow her to rest," Martha told them. "*Kumme* in and say hello and then you need to go back home with your *daed*."

Watching Ethan tape a piece of gauze over the spot on her arm where he'd drawn blood, Timothy's eyes bulged. "Did you have to get a shot, Trina?"

"Um, sort of. Dr. Gray had to use a needle to draw blood."

"Did it hurt?"

Ethan responded, "Trina was so brave she deserves two sugar-free lollipops." He held up the candy.

"I'm not hungry, but maybe you can give them to the *buwe*. They're usually pretty brave, too," Trina answered.

"Okay," Ethan agreed, "but first you have to promise me something, Timothy and Tanner. You have to be very helpful to whoever cares for you while Trina's asleep because she needs lots and lots of rest."

"Kind of like she's hibernating?" Timothy asked.

"Exactly like that." Ethan laughed, extending a lollipop to each of the boys.

"Starting now," Martha said. "It's time to hightail it, *buwe*."

"I'll be right out," Seth said as the others left the room.

He nervously pulled a chair to the side of

Trina's bed so his face was at the same level as hers. "I'm so sorry this happened," he said. The shadows beneath his eyes were so dark he looked as grim as she felt. Trina was overwhelmed by the depth of his concern.

"*You're* sorry? If you hadn't had to help me down from the rock, none of this would have happened. I'm the one who panicked about Tanner and ran into the water."

"That's what I love abo—" Seth coughed and started again. "That's what I appreciate. You put Tanner's welfare above your own. I can't ever express how much that means to me."

Was he going to say that's what he loved about me? Trina wondered. Or was she dreaming again? She must have been. After all, her eyes were closed and it seemed like she was floating. She hadn't felt this calm since before her mother got sick and if it was a dream, she didn't want to wake up from it for a long while.

When Seth exited Trina's room, Ethan was still in the kitchen with the others. He asked Seth if he'd walk to his car with him so they could talk and Seth obliged. He didn't know whether the serious look on Ethan's face was because he was concerned about Trina as a doctor, as a friend or possibly as a boyfriend.

"Are you sure she's going to be okay?" he asked anxiously before Ethan had a chance to speak.

"Trina? Yes, she should be fine. I'm running a few blood tests to make sure and I'll stop to check on her tomorrow. But I wanted to talk to you about your grandmother."

Seth was so surprised he repeated the *Englisch* term. "My grandmother?"

"Yes. I had a chance to speak with her about her vision and I believe she may have cataracts. There's a simple surgery she can have that will help restore her vision. It's important she has it soon, before the damage becomes irreversible."

Seth was taken aback. Who did Ethan think he was, questioning his grandmother about her health? Martha had accepted long ago she'd eventually go blind. For one thing, she believed it was God's will. For another, she was terrified of surgery. But a pushy *Englisch* doctor wouldn't understand that.

"*Denki* for caring for Trina on such short notice," Seth said pointedly ignoring Ethan's advice.

Ethan's features went slack. "As I said, I'll stop by tomorrow to see how she's doing. On Tuesday I won't be able to visit, since I'll be picking up my fiancée at the train station. She's coming from Philly during a break from her graduate studies. Her family lives close by so I'll get to spend some time with her, too."

His fiancée? Seth was more thrilled than he should have been to discover Ethan was engaged. The doctor gave him his card and said to call him or the hospital if Trina seemed confused, had a fever or was difficult to wake up.

When Seth returned to the house, Martha was sitting at the kitchen table with the boys, very quietly telling them the Bible story about Daniel in the lions' den. She tried to persuade Seth she'd be fine taking care of Trina overnight by herself, but this time he got the last word. He didn't want to have to worry about both her and Trina until morning.

"Maybe I can ask Emma Lamp if she'll spend the night tending to Trina. I could pay her for her assistance," he suggested.

Martha clucked and shook her head. "*Suh,* what you don't know about women could fill a book."

"What do you mean? Emma's helpful and capable, and there's a spare room here, so—"

"You know how word gets around in Willow Creek. Emma surely knows by now you chose to go out with Fannie again. Don't you think her feelings are hurt?"

"Why would Emma's feelings be hurt? Fannie didn't seem to mind I considered becoming Emma's suitor. I was very clear I wasn't making any definite commitments."

"Trust me, you can't ask Emma over." Martha paused and then instructed, "Here's what you need to do. Go to Pearl Hostetler's house and see if she'll *kumme* for the night. I'll bring the *buwe* back here with me in the morning. We'll do something quietly indoors for the day."

Seth had every intention of staying home the next day to watch the boys and help Martha with Trina's needs, but he didn't want to fight that battle at the moment. First, he had to secure help for that night. He felt funny burdening Pearl with assisting an *Englischer*, but he knew she wouldn't say no, in deference to Martha. Having been friends for over seventy years, the two women were like sisters and they'd do anything they could for each other.

After taking books and drawing paper back to Trina's house for the boys and stoking the fire, Seth left for Pearl's house. He worried she might be out visiting people instead of receiving visitors herself, so he was relieved when he arrived and Pearl answered the door.

"Seth, do *kumme* in. We were just talking about you. Rather, about your neighbor, Trina," Pearl bubbled, ushering him to the parlor without letting him get a word in edgewise. He wished she'd let him speak privately to her in the kitchen—this matter wasn't something he wanted to discuss in front of anyone else.

"Kate Dienner meet Seth Helmuth. You knew his *groossmammi*, Martha Helmuth, when you lived in Willow Creek. You might even remember his *daed,* Moses Helmuth, who lived here before he got married and moved to Ohio."

The woman, who looked to be a bit younger than his parents would have been, set down her cup and clasped her hands beneath her chin. "How *gut* to meet you, Seth. I do remember your *groossmammi,* but your *daed* was quite a few years older than I was, so I think by the time I went to school, he'd already moved to Ohio to marry your *mamm.* But Pearl tells me Patience Kauffman's daughter is living here now?"

Sometimes Seth wished everyone in Willow Creek didn't know everything about everyone else. No wonder Trina once told him living in the city afforded a person a certain amount of anonymity, which was sometimes beneficial. *"Jah,"* he said, wondering what else Pearl had told Kate.

"Patience and I were as thick as thieves until the summer I moved away when I was thirteen," Kate explained. "I haven't been back to

Willow Creek since then, but this week my husband has business in town. He's friends with Pearl and Wayne's son, so when they agreed to host us as while we're in town, we were delighted. Anyway, I'd love to meet Trina."

Seth waffled, "Um, I'm not sure that's a *gut* idea."

"It's alright," Kate assured him. "I know about how her *mamm* went *Englisch*. I'm not going to judge."

"*Neh*, it's not that," Seth said and then told them about their predicament. Kate insisted she should stay with Trina so Pearl could stay home to host both of their husbands. This actually seemed like a good idea to Seth, who was concerned about the older woman's stamina. Since Kate had only arrived the night before, she hadn't fully unpacked yet, so it only took a minute for her to gather her things and bid her husband goodbye at the barn where he was chatting with Pearl's husband, Wayne.

Back at Trina's house, Martha was just as glad to see Kate as Kate was to see her, and the older woman seemed relieved it was Kate, not Pearl, who would be staying the night with Trina.

"I'm here all week, so I can stay as long as you'd like," Kate said, but Seth supposed they'd only need her assistance for a night or maybe two.

Since Kate was so capable, the next day Seth decided that, rather than staying home, he'd take the boys with him to work so they'd be out of the women's way. It wouldn't be easy having them underfoot at the shop, but he had three *Englisch* customers coming to pick up their specialty orders and he didn't want to fail them if at all possible. First, he took Martha to Trina's house so she could keep Kate company, or more accurately, so Kate could keep an eye on Martha. While the boys waited outside, he popped in to ask about Trina.

"She had a slight fever last night, but nothing alarming. She's so exhausted I don't think she's even registered who I am. I'd like to stay another day, so if you could let Pearl and my husband know, I'd appreciate it."

"Will do," he agreed. "Is there anything I can bring you from town?"

"There sure is," Martha interrupted. "Half a dozen fry pies from the bakery."

When Seth raised an eyebrow, Martha said, "Unless you want me to bake, instead..." So he agreed to purchase the goodies.

As soon as the third customer had picked up her attaché case at two thirty, Seth closed shop. When he and the boys reached Trina's house, he noticed Ethan's car in the lane. Kate and Martha greeted them in the kitchen, just as Ethan emerged from Trina's room. He informed everyone that Trina's vitals seemed fine and her color was better now that she had rested.

"She's awake?" Seth asked.

"She sure is. She's hungry, too. You can go through and see her if you'd like. She's dressed and she wants to come out for something to eat and to sit by the fire. She might need a hand for balance."

The door was ajar but Seth knocked anyway and slowly pushed it open when Trina told him to come in. She was sitting on the edge of the bed, which was made, with a hairbrush in her hand, but her tresses were still loose.

"Hi, Trina. How are you?" he asked.

"Seth! You're home early. It's because you couldn't get someone to care for the *buwe*, isn't it?"

"Well, I wouldn't blame anyone for not wanting to. After all, look what happens when someone does care for them," he said, gesturing toward her in reference to her illness.

But she must have misinterpreted his comment, because she tucked her hair behind her ear. "I know I look a mess. I can't believe a simple thing like combing my hair requires so much energy today."

"*Neh*, I meant, look what happens to your health, not to your hair," Seth protested. Then, although he knew he shouldn't give voice to his thoughts, he didn't stop himself from adding, "Your hair always looks pretty, whether it's around your shoulders or pulled up in a horse's tail."

Trina threw back her head. Seth wasn't sure how she'd take the compliment, but he hadn't expected her to laugh at it. "You mean a *pony*-tail," she said, and then he had to laugh, too.

"Everyone is in the kitchen preparing sweets and waiting to see you. Can I help you up?" Seth offered his arm and Trina grasped it as she pulled herself into a standing position. Then she let go and took a few wobbly steps. Seth immediately held out his hand again and she interlocked her fingers with his. They simultaneously lowered their arms between them as if they were holding hands while out for a stroll. The sensation made *him* feel unsteady but he ambled with her down the hallway like that. Then, squeezing their fingers in silent agreement, right before entering the kitchen they released each other's hand so no one would see.

* * *

Seth's steady, masculine fingers gripping hers for a few fleeting seconds was worth every hour of feeling lousy the past night and day. Trina hadn't glanced at him while they were walking hand in hand from her room down the short hallway and through the parlor because she hadn't wanted to discover she was having another feverish dream. But once the warmth of his skin against hers slipped away and she entered the brightness of the kitchen, she knew it had been real and she wished she had walked slower. Or stopped walking altogether—anything to prolong their closeness.

She'd been close to Seth before, of course, such as when he'd helped her down from the rock or up from her bed, but this time was different; this time there was no questioning whether there was something more than helpfulness or friendliness between them. Right before dropping her hand, Seth had given hers a squeeze and she'd squeezed back in secret acknowledgment of their mutual affection.

So when Martha told her she looked dazed, Trina replied, "I'm fine. It's just I'm not used to the bright sunlight," and the woman introduced as Kate Dienner quickly drew the shade.

After the boys had given her drawings of lions they made while they were at Seth's shop,

Kate poured tea for the adults and milk for the boys, and then served apple fry pies.

"What about me? Don't I get one?" Trina sounded like a disappointed child when she wasn't offered a piece of dessert.

"I don't know if that's wise, dear," Martha said. "I think you should start slowly, maybe have a piece of dry toast."

Trina wrinkled her nose. "Dry toast?" she repeated, as if she'd been offered a dead skunk. "I've been exhausted, not sick to my stomach."

Seth interjected, "Before he left, Dr. Gray— I mean, Ethan—didn't say she couldn't have regular food, so I don't see any harm in it."

Trina glanced at him and said, "*Jah*, please listen to the man who thinks I need to fatten up." The second the words were out of her mouth she worried her comment indicated they'd been bantering in a way that might not have been considered appropriate for an Amish man and an *Englisch* woman.

Fortunately, Timothy piped up. "*Jah, Groossmammi*. When bears *kumme* out of hibernation, they're hungry, too, and they forage for food."

"You don't have to forage, Trina." Tanner offered, "You can have mine."

Clearly the darling boy still felt guilty for

Trina's incident at the creek and her heart expanded to near bursting from his sentiment.

Martha chuckled. "Alright, alright. But don't blame me if you get a tummy ache," she said as if Trina were a youngster.

The fry pies were so delicious Trina said, "This is the best thing I've ever tasted. And that's not just because I'm ravenous." As she licked icing from her upper lip, she caught Seth looking at her and he quickly glanced away again.

"We should go, *buwe*," he said when they'd all finished eating, and Martha agreed.

After they left, Kate insisted Trina sit down in the parlor and Trina was suddenly so tired again that she didn't argue. After Kate finished washing the cups and glasses, she brought Trina a drink of water, urging her to increase her intake of liquids.

"*Denki* for staying with me," Trina said. "I don't know how to express my appreciation that you'd do this for a stranger."

"Anyone who lives in Willow Creek isn't a stranger," Kate replied, settling onto the sofa opposite. "And you especially aren't a stranger. I grew up with your *mamm*. At least, until I was about thirteen and we moved away."

Trina's concentration must have been off due to her illness because she couldn't place the woman in the stories her mother shared. The only childhood friend she mentioned had the last name of Stuckey, not Dienner. And her first name was Katrina, not Kate. Suddenly, it dawned on Trina, "What was your name before you married?"

"Stuckey," Kate said.

Trina leaped up so quickly she felt unsteady again. "You're Katrina Stuckey!" she exclaimed.

Kate moved to Trina's side and eased her onto the sofa beside her. *"Jah,"* she said. "Although Patience was the only person I ever allowed to call me by my full name, Katrina. Everyone else calls me Kate."

"My *mamm* thought the world of you. That's why she named me Trina." Trina didn't know if it was because she'd been sick, but she was suddenly overwhelmed with emotion and she began to weep into her hands.

Kate wrapped her arm around Trina's shoulder. "I know. I know," she said soothingly, until Trina caught her breath again. Then she told her, "Patience was such a dear *maedel*, my closest friend. How I regret losing touch with her after I moved…"

It was Trina's turn to comfort the older woman. "*Mamm* understood. She said she figured you were probably adjusting to life with your new friends in a new place and she wanted you to be happy there." After a pause, Trina confided, "My *mamm* left the Amish, you know."

"I do know. I probably even know why," Kate said. "I might not agree with her decision, but I really do understand why she made it."

Trina changed the subject to something happier. "One of *mamm*'s favorite memories was when the two of you went ice skating on her thirteen birthday at Wheeler's Pond the winter before you moved."

"Mine, too! Our teeth were chattering and our toes were frozen, but we didn't want to leave. Not as long as the *buwe* were still playing broom hockey."

"What?" Trina's mother hadn't told Trina about that.

"*Jah*—we were awfully young, but your *mamm* was smitten with a boy named Hannes Kinnell and I liked Jethro Bechler. That's why Patience decided the perfect birthday would be spent trying to capture their attention. We even brought a thermos of cocoa to entice them to chat with us." Kate shook her head, remembering.

"Did they?"

"Only long enough to drink the cocoa." Kate giggled. "Now I don't blame them. They were a *gut* five years older than we were. Mind you, they were decent *buwe* and kind in their own way, but they weren't interested in us romantically at all. But, at the time, we were devastated. I think both of them eventually married *meed* from Ohio. And I married a man from Indiana."

"And my *mamm* married an *Englischer* from New York," Trina said sadly.

"I always hoped she had met someone like Hannes," Kate said. "I'm sure if she'd met a man like that, she never would have left the Amish."

"That may be true," Trina agreed. "Sometimes, growing up, I felt like she didn't leave the Amish—she only left the geography. I mean, she was still true to her faith. She was true to me, as her family. And she passed down so many Amish ideals and traditions." Trina laughed. "She tried to, anyway. Some of them I didn't want to learn. Like how to wash the windows until they sparkled."

"To tell you the truth, I still don't like washing windows," Kate said, laughing.

The conversation was bittersweet and Trina felt worn out with emotion and from the increase in activity, so she decided to turn in early that evening. Kate helped her get ready for bed and brought her a glass of water.

"I always wondered what your *mamm* would look like if I saw her again as an adult," she confessed. "I used to wonder if I'd recognize her. Now that I've seen you, I know I would have. There's a lot of her in you, Trina. As much as you miss her, you have so many of her ways."

Trina was glad it was too dark for Kate to see her tears. *"Denki,"* she murmured.

But when the door closed behind Kate, Trina couldn't sleep. She thought about how Kate had said that if Trina's mother had found a kind and honest man like Hannes Kinnell, she probably wouldn't have left the Amish. Seth was a kind and decent man, but Trina couldn't become Amish to have a romantic relationship with him. Being Amish was about a commitment to God, first and foremost. Yet she kept thinking, *But I already have that commitment to the Lord. It would just be a different way of demonstrating it.* Then she asked herself, if Seth continued to court and even married Fannie, would Trina still want to become Amish? She wasn't quite sure, although there was definitely something about being among the *leit* of Willow Creek that made her feel as if she'd come home.

Which in turn made her feel guilty. Like a traitor. How could she think of returning to the place her mother fled from? What kind of daughter was she? No, in her weakened state, her mind was playing tricks on her. She knew she needed rest, and before she could even roll over in bed, she'd fallen asleep again.

Because Martha absolutely wouldn't take no for an answer, Seth reluctantly agreed to leave the boys home with her the following day.

"I promise not to use the stove or oven," she said. "If I want tea, I'll drop in on Kate. This will mean you'll have to get a pizza for dinner."

"Pizza!" Timothy and Tanner cheered. Takeout pizza was a rare treat in their house and he was glad his sons were so happy about it. Tanner had seemed unusually out of sorts since Trina's creek incident, even though Seth repeatedly assured him it wasn't his fault.

"*Daed*, I told Fannie where I'd be," he explained. "I don't know why she said she couldn't find me."

Seth had suspected as much. Fannie had probably beckoned Seth because she didn't want him to be alone with Trina any longer than he had been. Seth sighed, knowing she probably had good reason to be wary of the two of them dawdling behind. Every fiber of his being had wanted to take Trina's hand and run in the opposite direction that day.

Thinking about Trina's fingers interlocked with his in the hallway of her house made Seth sore with yearning. There was no denying they had joined hands the way a couple would and held on until the last possible second. It was so romantic how, as they let go, her fingers delicately trailed along his palm and his trailed along hers until just their fingertips were touching before they'd parted contact completely. Ordinarily, the Amish didn't prohibit handholding before marriage. But a baptized Amish man handholding with an *Englischer*, when marriage wasn't even possible, was another story. Seth knew he was in a precarious position, but at that moment he hadn't cared. If he had to do it all over again, he would have.

A deep ache harried him all through the morning in his shop. It was a mix of longing and guilt, as well as a strange new understanding of his brother. For the first time since Freeman left, Seth experienced an inkling of empathy toward him, even though he didn't agree with the choices his brother ultimately made. It was bad enough that Freeman brought pain to their family, but if Seth were to leave, it would be that much worse because he had children. He couldn't imagine tearing them away from their Amish roots—making a choice for them he hoped they'd never make for themselves.

What was wrong with him to even entertain the notion of leaving the Amish? *I could never do that*, he thought. *I've got to put these feelings about Trina aside*. That's all they were—feelings. Emotions. Whims. Besides, she was leaving soon. Was Seth going to ruin his reputation by flirting with an *Englischer* who was just passing through?

Of course he wasn't. But try as he might, he still couldn't get thoughts of Trina out of his mind. He thought of her telling him she'd always have the memory of her mother and herself at the Cape to hold on to. Likewise, Seth would always have the memory of holding hands with Trina, as forbidden as it was. But no, that wouldn't do. It would be wrong to harbor such a thought.

Instead, he decided to help Trina safeguard *her* memory of her mother in a material sense. He wanted to fashion a picture frame made of leather. But first he walked to the library on his dinner break and checked out a book on birds. Using the index, he located the page that contained a picture of sandpipers. Yes, that's what he'd etch into the leather along the border of the frame: two sandpipers scurrying along the edge of a wave. One for Trina and one for her mother. Far, far from here.

It would be his parting gift to Trina, so she wouldn't forget him, since she wasn't forbidden to dwell on the memories of their time together. As for him, he had to put thoughts of her out of his mind for good.

"Can Trina eat supper with us?" Timothy asked when Seth arrived home that night carrying a big square box of pizza.

"*Neh*, she's eating with Kate at her house tonight."

"Pearl stopped by to check on Trina and Kate. Since Ethan visited today and said Trina was much better, Pearl took Kate back to her house. So I think Trina would *wilkom* a chance to eat with us," Martha suggested.

"This pizza isn't very big," Seth argued.

"What has gotten into you, *suh*?" Martha asked. When he didn't answer she said, "Alright, fine. I'll go over to Trina's house and make supper for her there."

"*Neh!*" Seth barked the word at his grandmother. Why couldn't she just leave well enough alone? It was futile; she'd never change. "I'm sorry. I didn't mean to snap, *Groossmammi*. I mean *neh*, it's dark. I'll walk over and get her. I don't want you to fall."

Martha looked dubious but since she'd gotten her way, she said, "*Kumme, buwe*, help me put plates and napkins on the table."

"Pizza sounds *appenditlich*," Trina said, accepting Seth's invitation after he knocked on her door. Her hair was neatly arranged in a bun and she was wearing the skirt she'd been sewing with Martha's guidance.

"I see you're wearing the skirt you made," he said and immediately regretted it. She might think he was too preoccupied with her appearance. Which he was.

"*Jah*, but I had to move the button. In fact, I've had to move the buttons on all of my skirts," she said. "I've actually gained a few pounds since I arrived here."

"That's *gut*," he said as he hurried down the porch steps and along the walkway, not wishing to get too close to her again.

From behind, Trina called, "I'm sorry. I'm still a little weak. I can't keep up."

Seth slowed his pace. He couldn't look at her for fear the hole in his heart would grow even bigger.

"Is something wrong?" she asked when she caught up. "You seem distracted."

Seth stopped to face her. He loved how tall she was, how he could look her in the eyes. "I'm sorry, Trina. For yesterday. I shouldn't have and I'm sorry."

"Shouldn't have what?" she asked. Was she being coy? Or hadn't she felt what he felt? No, he couldn't believe that, even if she was going to make him say it aloud.

"I'm sorry for holding your hand like I did. I shouldn't have done that and I promise you it won't ever happen again."

Trina stumbled backward as if she'd been struck and her mouth fell open. Then she turned on her heel.

"Trina, wait!"

She whirled back around and in the dimming light he noticed her cheeks suddenly glistened with tears. "I understand, Seth, why you and I can never be... I understand that you're Amish and I'm *Englisch*. But I'm not sorry about the affection you've shown me. And I'm not sorry you know I feel the same way about you."

Watching her dash back toward her house, Seth fought the impulse to follow her and profess his affection—his *love*—too. Letting her go was the most difficult thing he'd ever done and when the door closed behind her, he dropped to his knees, covered his face with his arm and groaned in a way he hadn't since he was in mourning.

Chapter Eight

In the weeks following her illness, Trina went out of her way to avoid Seth, and it appeared he was avoiding her, too. It would have been painful enough if they'd kept their distance because they were having an argument, but this time, Trina knew it was because they *weren't* having an argument. They were keeping their distance because they both knew how dear they were to each other and they couldn't act on those feelings.

Trina tried to force herself into cheerfulness, but even her best experiences with the boys were tinged with the awareness she'd soon leave them. Of course, the change in her mood didn't escape Martha's notice, nor did the change in her relationship with Seth. One Friday night when Trina and Seth were alone in the kitchen after having supper—Martha had insisted Trina eat with them since Seth had returned home so late that day—he handed her a plate by the sink. He was in such a rush to get away from her he didn't wait until her fingers had wholly grasped the dish and it slipped and shattered on the floor.

Martha flew into the kitchen, nearly toppling a chair one of the boys had pulled away from the table so he could sweep the floor beneath it. "What is going on?" she demanded.

"I'm sorry. I dropped a dish," Seth said before Trina could take the blame for it.

"I'll clean it up," Trina quickly offered.

"*Neh*, you'll do no such thing," Martha scolded. She had an edge to her voice Trina hadn't heard directed at her before. "The two of you will clean up whatever disagreement you've had before you'll tend to a few bits of broken glass."

"We haven't had a disagreement," Seth objected.

"Don't give me that. You've both been sulking like wet *katze*. The tension is almost unbearable. I can't stand it in my house a moment longer and neither can the *buwe*. So go outside until you can *kumme* back reconciled and smiling." Martha pointed to the door. She meant business.

Trina quietly dried her hands and lifted her

light sweater from the peg by the door. The mid-April evening air was just chilly enough for her to need it, although Seth didn't bother to put on his jacket. Trina walked to the railing and burst into tears. She didn't mean to, but Martha was right; the tension was unbearable. She couldn't contain it any longer.

"Trina, please don't cry," Seth said, but he didn't draw near. His tone was so kind it made her cry even harder. "I wish I could make this better, but I don't know what to do," he said, walking to the railing but staying at least four feet away from Trina. What was he afraid of? It was insulting that he didn't even trust her enough to stand by her side. Or maybe it was himself he didn't trust. Maybe, instead of bridging the distance between them, they needed to increase it even more—for his good, as well as hers. Clearly he was hurting, too.

"I do," she sighed, drying her eyes on the edge of her apron. "It's only a couple more weeks until my time here is up. I'd considered staying until the house is sold and watching the *buwe* until school lets out at the end of May, but I think I should leave on May first, instead."

Seth ran his hand through his hair and tipped his head toward the sky. Was that a tear he wiped from his face when he brought his hand down to his side again? "*Jah*, that's probably for the best," he admitted. In a lower voice he said, as if speaking to himself, "Even though it feels like it's for the worst."

Just hearing him acknowledge how difficult it was to separate moved Trina deeply. He was obviously upset and she wished she could allay his suffering. They were both silent, observing the dusky spring sky. It would have seemed romantic under any other circumstances but this evening Trina had to concentrate on practical matters. "Until I leave, we've got to convince Martha there's nothing wrong between us."

Seth shrugged. "I don't know if we can. Nothing gets by her."

"Nonsense!" Trina declared, sounding just like Martha herself. "If your *buwe* can pretend they're wolves, then you and I can pretend nothing's wrong."

"It would be easier to pretend I'm a wolf," Seth muttered, and then he quietly howled toward the rising moon, causing them both to laugh.

"*Kumme,*" Trina said, motioning toward the door. "We can do it. For the *buwe*'s sake. I don't want them to remember our time together as being tense."

Seth agreed and when they opened the

kitchen door, Martha was standing there with a broom. "All better?" she demanded.

"All better," they both claimed at the same time.

"*Gut*. Then Seth can sweep up the glass and Trina, you serve dessert. The *buwe* want to play Noah's Ark again. I think it's time for you to teach them a new game, Trina. I'm getting tired of guessing they're bears, wolves or tigers."

So when they finished eating dessert, Trina told Timothy and Tanner that Martha would be Noah and the boys had to be Noah's sons, while Seth and Trina acted out the animals. Their imitations were humorously awful and everyone laughed so hard Trina's smile came naturally again.

The next day was Saturday, and after Seth returned from work, Trina went home to call the realtor from church Sherman and Mabel had recommended. She forgot she'd put the phone back in Abe's old bedroom and she was glad to discover it was set on vibrate. She would have regretted if it had rung while Kate was sleeping there. Exiting the room, Trina noticed a Bible on the nightstand. Was that Abe's or did Kate forget hers there? She picked it up to see whose name was inscribed in it; it was her grandfather's. As she was putting the Bible back on the nightstand, an envelope fell from its pages. TRINA it said in big letters. It must have been from Kate; perhaps she'd written down more memories of Patience she wanted to share with Trina.

Deciding she'd be too emotional to make her phone call if she read the letter first, Trina set the envelope on the end table in the parlor and then turned her attention to her cell phone. It logged thirteen unanswered calls. Thirteen! All from Kurt, the realtor. Suddenly, she was infuriated. Seth was right, *Englischers* were pushy. Kurt just wouldn't take no for an answer. Trina pressed his number in her call history setting and paced while she was waiting for him to pick up. When he did, she didn't give him any time to work his sales pitch on her.

"This is Trina Smith and I want you to stop calling me," she spouted. "I will never, ever sell my house to a land developer. If I have to, I'll make it a stipulation of sale that any new owner can only resell to an Amish resident for the next one hundred years!" She was about to disconnect but she wanted to wait until Kurt confirmed he'd heard her loud and clear.

"You're saying you wouldn't sell to anyone who isn't Amish?" he asked.

Trina didn't know if such a stipulation was

even legally allowed, but she confirmed, "That's exactly what I'm saying."

"Not even if the buyer is your father, Richard Smith?"

Trina staggered backward and dropped onto the sofa. "My father? Is this some kind of joke?"

"It's not a joke at all, Trina. How do you think I knew you had a house for sale? Your father contacted me and told me all about it."

"How did *he* know?" Trina asked suspiciously.

"He tried to track you down after your mother died and eventually his inquiries led him to Willow Creek, where rumors spread like wildfire."

Trina couldn't deny how quickly gossip traveled through the tiny community. "Why would my father want to buy a house—my *mother's* house—here?"

"He wants to reconnect with you, Trina. He wants to be part of your life again. Taking the house off your hands would be a way for him to help you out."

That didn't sound like her father. He had never tried to help her when she was a child and at her most vulnerable. Why would he help her now? "What's in it for him?" she asked.

Kurt coughed. "Well, he's sort of taken a

hit recently, with the economy and the stock market… He sees this as an opportunity to get back on his feet. He's afraid he's going to lose his own house and wind up on the street."

Trina hadn't known that, but hearing it now filled her with conflicting emotions. Her first thought was of her mother. It didn't seem fair that her father was griping about losing his house when Trina's mother had never owned a house herself. Half the time, she'd struggled just to pay rent.

Yet Trina was also choked up to learn her father might be on the brink of homelessness. She didn't want to turn her back on him, even though he had neglected to help Trina and her mother for years. Regardless, Patience had frequently urged Trina not to bear a grudge against him. "God is forgiving and he wants us to be forgiving, too," she'd say. "For our sake as well as for the other person's sake. Remember, bitterness harms us more than it harms anyone else."

"My father wants to move here?" Trina asked Kurt. It didn't make sense. She couldn't imagine her father living next door to Seth. More importantly, she couldn't imagine her father living in her mother's childhood home. It wasn't right; somehow, it seemed like a betrayal.

"Not exactly." From the length of his pause

Trina knew Kurt was going to tell her something she didn't want to hear. "Uh, remember the developer I told you about? Well, the developer is actually your father. And he's, um, partnering with a business associate who can front the cost of buying your house…"

Trina felt as if she'd been knocked flat to be told her father was the one behind the proposal to use the property for a liquor store. She didn't even have to think about her response. "No. Absolutely not."

"Don't you care if your father ends up bankrupt and homeless?"

"Of course I care," Trina said. "But that doesn't mean I'll sell him the house and land. Please don't call me again. This matter is closed."

Her emotions roiling, Trina's hands trembled as she disconnected the call. She knew her refusal to sell to her father might mean he'd suffer financial hardship. No matter what he'd done—or what he *hadn't* done—in the past, Trina still regretted letting him down now. As her mother had always reminded her, for better or worse, he was the only father she had.

But she couldn't in good conscience allow the property to be used for a liquor store. To do so would add insult to injury in regard to her mother's past. Not to mention, the presence of a wine and spirits store in a residential location would be a violation of the values of Willow Creek's Amish community, especially the Helmuths. Suspecting Kurt would continue to hound her despite her refusal, Trina figured the only way to get him to back off would be to sell to someone else as soon as possible. Picking up the phone, she called the realtor from her church as quickly as her fingers could tap the numbers.

Seeing Emma Lamp at church always made Seth feel that much worse about his future. He knew he couldn't court Trina, for obvious reasons. But each time he saw Emma he realized he couldn't court her or Fannie or anyone else for a reason that had now become crystal clear: he couldn't imagine himself growing to love another woman. Rather, he knew he'd never be *in* love with anyone the way he was in love with Trina. Knowing her had changed what was acceptable to him for a marriage relationship. Loving her had been effortless; it was *not* loving her that was going to be a struggle. From now on, he'd stay single and pay a nanny to mind the boys and help Martha rather than marry someone he didn't love.

"Can we ask Trina to walk to the creek with

us?" Tanner asked when they arrived home after church and Martha had turned in for a nap.

"*Jah*, she hasn't caught a frog yet," Timothy pleaded. "She hasn't even seen any tadpoles."

"Okay," Seth agreed. It was exactly two weeks before May first, the day Trina would move, and he realized the boys wanted to spend as much time with her as possible. "You go knock on her door and invite her and I'll wait here beneath the willow."

The yard had come alive; green buds decorated the willow, yellow daffodils shone like sunshine along the lane and Martha's tulips had overtaken the garden in a variety of purples, pinks and reds. But Seth's appreciation of spring dimmed in comparison with how he felt when he glimpsed Trina walking toward him, her long hair loose and glinting in the sun, the boys frolicking at her side. But when she came close, Seth saw her nostrils were pink and she was wearing the mirrored glasses she'd loaned Martha so long ago.

"*Buwe*, you run to that big rock over there and climb up on it to make sure you don't see any birds of prey around, okay? I need to talk to your *daed*."

Seth held his breath. If Trina cried in front of him one more time, he might break down and take her into his arms.

"I have to tell you something about my *daed*," she began, and he released his breath. So it wasn't about him—about *them*—after all. Yet, as she told him about her father contacting the realtor and how he was the developer who wanted to build a liquor store, Seth had to fight twice as hard not to embrace her. He could hear how distressed she was that her father might be facing financial ruin. How could a father manipulate his daughter's emotions for financial gain?

"My *daed* never honored a single commitment to help provide for me when I was a *kin*," Trina confided. "My *mamm* had to scrimp and save and work two or three menial jobs at a time. As I've mentioned, we were often very poor. I didn't care about that as much as I cared about my *daed* never following through with his promises. He'd say he'd *kumme* visit me and I'd get my hopes up, but then he wouldn't show…and other things like that. After a while, I lost faith in him altogether. But *mamm* was never bitter. Before she died, she told me if my *daed* ever tried to reconcile with me, she hoped I'd give him another chance. She said she didn't want my relationship with him to be estranged like hers was with her own *daed*."

Seth's fingers were curled into fists. "But

your father hasn't actually asked for your forgiveness, has he?"

"*Neh*, not exactly. But the realtor said he wanted to reconnect with me. I don't know if he's sincere or if he's just after my inheritance. But that's not the point. The point is it was important to my *mamm* that I allow him back into my life if he wants to reconcile. And the Lord desires us to be forgiving, too."

"I understand," Seth said solemnly, marveling at Trina's willingness to honor her mother's wishes, as well as to obey God's word about forgiveness.

"Of course, forgiving him and allowing him back into my life doesn't mean selling the property to him," Trina clarified. "If he's truly desperate, perhaps I can help him financially so he doesn't end up homeless. I've contacted a realtor from church and I've asked about making a quick sale so no one can pressure me. We also discussed putting conditions on ownership, so no one can turn around and sell the house to anyone except residents in the future, too."

The gravity of what Trina had done sank in for Seth. Not only was she honoring her mother's memory, but she'd rejected her father's offer in favor of the Amish. She no doubt would have profited greatly from selling the property to him, but she'd said no in part because she understood the adverse effect a liquor store in that area would have on Seth and his family, as well as on the rest of the Amish community. Just when he thought he couldn't love her any more…

"Trina," he said, touching her arm gently. "Please take off those sunglasses and look at me. I need to see your eyes."

Trina did as he asked and gazed at him, droplets collecting on her lashes.

"I can never repay what you've done for my family and me. For all of Willow Creek's Amish. What you're doing takes courage and—" Seth's voice cracked and he abruptly stopped talking and tried to regain his composure.

"Denki," Trina uttered, blinking. Then she cleared her throat and said pointedly, "It was the right decision, but sometimes even making the right decision is difficult. It's excruciating."

Seth nodded, knowing what she meant. She was talking about the two of them parting ways because it was the right thing for each of them to do.

"Trina! *Daed!* Why are you just standing there like that?" Tanner called from atop of the large rock in the distance.

Timothy was more polite. "Please *kumme*! If

you don't hurry all the tadpoles will be grown up by the time we get to the creek."

The two adults chuckled, in spite of themselves. Trina glanced sideways at Seth and taunted, "I'll beat you there."

"Don't be so sure about that," Seth retorted, breaking into a run.

Several paces later, Trina passed him, her hair flying out behind her as Timothy and Tanner cheered them on. She tagged the rock before Seth did and then collapsed onto her back on the new grass, laughing and clutching her stomach. The boys scrambled down to pull her up by her hands, just as they had that first day. It was the only moment in his life when Seth ever wished he had a camera so he could capture the sight on film as well as in his memory.

Trina had been so distraught about Kurt's phone call on Saturday that she completely forgot about the envelope with her name on it until midway through the week. She was cleaning her house on Wednesday morning because the realtor, Dianne Barrett, had said she'd come over later that day while Martha watched the boys. The meeting with Dianne was really just a formality since Trina had already spoken to her about making a quick sale and about the stipulation of the property being family owned for any sales within the next fifty years.

Trina tucked the envelope into her nightstand drawer so she could read it at bedtime and then she surveyed the house. Aside from the surface cracks Seth had fixed, it was a sturdy, well-built home and she hoped the realtor could find a nice, quiet but friendly couple or small family to make it their home. Seth had said he'd ask Amish families to spread the word to their relatives in neighboring districts. Perhaps one of them would want to relocate to Willow Creek. *As long as it's not Fannie Jantzi*, Trina thought. *Because I don't believe she's given up on Seth so easily.*

Trina should know; she was still having a hard time letting go of him herself. She was so depressed about it her appetite vanished again and she spent more time awake than asleep at night. Despite her insomnia, Trina forced herself to go through the motions of a regular routine, just as she had after her mother died. For the sake of the boys—and to make things easier on Seth—she was determined to keep her feelings about leaving to herself, too. There would be enough time to cry after she returned to Philadelphia.

But who would help comfort her there? Missing her mother had been more bearable when Trina was surrounded by people who knew her and could bring memories of her to mind. But because Patience and Trina had moved around so frequently and her mother tended to keep to herself, there was no one in the *Englisch* world who could comfort Trina as well as the Amish had comforted her, even if their memories were only of Patience when she was a girl.

By the time Seth returned home that evening, Trina was beat and she declined Martha's invitation to eat supper with them. Remembering the envelope from Kate and hoping it contained memories about her mother, Trina went to bed early so she could savor reading it beneath the covers. She delicately tore the envelope open and unfolded the paper. The letter was longer than she expected and as she scanned the page, she was aghast to realize the signature was Abe Kauffman's. Her hands trembled as she read.

Dear Trina,
You probably know a little about me from stories your mother told you. Regrettably, they're all true. I was exactly the kind of father she said I was. Actually, knowing her kindness, I was probably much worse than Patience ever described.

It's not an excuse for my behavior, but after your grandmother died, part of me died, too. Instead of cherishing my daughter and relying on Gott for comfort, I turned to drinking, may the Lord forgive me.

You're probably also aware that your mother sent me a photo of you with a brief letter every year until you turned eighteen. What you don't know is how much her messages meant to me. I've kept them and the photos in the drawer in my nightstand if you want them.

Trina sat straight up in bed. It felt as if her world was tipping on its axis. She had no idea her mother had communicated with Abe for eighteen years, much less sent him photos of Trina. She didn't know what to make of this new information. Why wouldn't her mother have told her she'd done that? She continued reading.

Her sweet letters might be of consolation now that Patience is with the Lord instead of with you, just as they were a comfort to me when she was in the *Englisch* world instead of with the Amish community.

This part of the letter made Trina so furious she would have liked to rip the letter to shreds. The nerve of him! He was the very reason Trina's mother left the Amish. What right did he have to claim he missed her?

As you'll read, after your father divorced her, your mother asked me each year to say the word and she'd return with you to Willow Creek. But I couldn't. I wouldn't. And I want you to know why because it had nothing to do with her or you or with being Amish.

Now Trina started to cry. Was Abe lying? She felt as if she didn't even know her mother anymore. She'd had no idea Patience had so much as thought about returning home, much less asked for Abe's approval to do so. Every time she'd talked to her mother about going back to Willow Creek, her mother said they were better off where they were. Why would Patience lie to her about something so important?

Then Trina realized her mother hadn't actually ever said she wasn't in contact with her family. Whenever Trina asked her if she wanted to go back, her mother had replied, "You don't understand, honey. That's just not done under circumstances like mine."

"It isn't? Not ever?"

"Well, there is a process which allows a person to repent and return. But for someone who is divorced…well, there's a great deal of shame in that."

Trina had always assumed her mother was talking about her own shame. Now it was dawning on her that Patience had longed to return, but she wouldn't because she wanted to spare Abe the shame of having a divorced runaway daughter. Trina sat there weeping for some time before she could read any further.

To say I wanted my daughter to come back would be to admit I was the reason she left in the first place. That would mean coming to terms with my drinking, which I was unwilling to do.

As contradictory as this sounds, I was ashamed of myself. I read Patience's letters and saw the photos of you and I knew your mother was raising you far better than I ever raised her. I thought you'd be happier in the *Englisch* world with her than you'd ever be within a one-hundred-mile radius of me.

It wasn't until I stopped drinking four years ago that I began to take responsibility for my wrongdoings. By then, the letters had stopped coming and I figured Patience no longer wanted to return home. I tried several times to locate you two, but my letters were returned with a stamp indicating you'd moved. Smith is a common name so I couldn't track you down after that.

I didn't hear about you and Patience again until your father contacted me and informed me of her passing.

So, Trina's father *had* known about Patience's death. Why hadn't he at least gotten in touch with Trina to offer consolation? Hadn't he been able to find her, either?

To say how grieved I was would be an insult to your own grief.

That's for sure! Trina thought and then she kept reading.

But I want you to know I am so sorry for your loss. Your mother loved you dearly and I'm sure you loved her dearly, too.

People often said Patience made the decision to leave the Amish, but in truth, I didn't give her much of a choice. I feel like I've stolen an opportunity from you as well as from her, which is why I put the stipulation on the inheritance that you have to stay here for sixty days. I want you to decide for yourself whether you want to live in Willow Creek.

Your mother gave you the best parts of being Amish—her faith and her love. But she couldn't give you the community. For what it's worth, I want to give you that now.

Whether or not you choose to stay in Willow Creek, I pray you'll forgive me. I wish I had said those words to your mother, too, but I trust we'll be reconciled in heaven, through God's grace.

Abraham Kauffman
PS: I've had a problem with mice. The next-door neighbor, Seth Helmuth, might be able to trap them for you if you're squeamish.

Despite her heartache, Trina laughed aloud at the postscript, but the laughter twisted deep within her chest, like a sob. Too distraught get up and retrieve the photos and letters from the drawer in Abe's old room, she curled up in a ball, alternately thinking, weeping and praying for guidance until the sun came up.

When Seth returned from milking the cow on Thursday morning, he noticed the kitchen lamp on and he smelled something baking in the oven, but his grandmother wasn't present.

"Groossmammi?" he said quietly, wiping his boots on the rag rug by the door. When she didn't answer, he walked toward the parlor, but she wasn't there, either.

"I'm here," a muffled voice cried from the hall.

When Seth came around the corner, he spotted her sitting on the floor with her back against the wall and he rushed to her side. "Are you hurt?"

"I don't think so. Help me up, slowly, please."

Seth cautiously eased her to a standing position and she moaned as she limped toward the sofa with his assistance. Then he settled her onto a cushion.

"That's better," she said. "I'll sit here awhile. Will you bring me my *kaffi*?"

Seth retrieved the steaming cup and only then did he ask what happened.

"I don't know. I slipped on something, I guess."

Seth walked to the hall and looked. One of

the boys' library books lay on the floor. How many times had he told them to put their books away at night? Yet he wasn't really angry at them; he was upset that such a small thing could have resulted in a big accident for his grandmother.

"Are you certain you're okay?" he asked again. "You didn't bump your head, did you?"

"*Neh*. I caught myself before my head hit. My arm hurts a little, but it was probably from the impact."

But Seth continued to worry about her until Trina arrived and he pulled her aside to tell her what happened.

"Oh, *neh*!" she exclaimed, which elicited a scolding from Martha in the other room.

"You two need to stop talking about me in there. I told you I'm fine."

Trina whispered, "She probably *is* fine but should we take her to the hospital to get checked out?"

"She hates hospitals. She wouldn't go," Seth answered. He didn't add, "And I wouldn't, either."

"Perhaps you could ask Ethan if he'd take a look. She seems to like him alright."

Seth agreed but instead of using the phone shanty he decided on his way to the shop he'd stop and talk to Ethan in person at his home.

The doctor seemed glad to help before going to the clinic. "I want to see Trina as often as I can before she goes back to Philly, anyway."

His reminder that Trina was leaving soon was like a punch to Seth's gut, but he thanked Ethan and continued toward work. It was pouring and it took him longer than usual to get there. On the way he thought about what could have happened to Martha. He couldn't put it off: he definitely needed someone to keep her safe as much as he needed someone to watch the boys. What was he going to do in between the time Trina left, and school let out and a local *maedel* was available? Would it really be so offensive if he asked Emma Lapp to help? His understanding was she didn't have a full-time job until the summer when her family sold produce at their roadside vegetable stand.

Inside the shop, he examined the leather frame he'd made for Trina. He just had to burn a few more details of the etching before it would be ready to give to her, but since it was a parting gift he delayed finishing it, as if that would mean she wasn't leaving. Once again, thinking about her departure made his stomach hurt and he was unusually irritable with a customer because her coat dripped rain onto one of the suede purses he had on display.

Then, as if his day couldn't get any worse, at two o'clock Fannie Jantzi came by with Hope and Greta. "We were buying cupcakes for Greta's birthday at the bakery," she explained.

Seth was surprised—Elmsville to Willow Creek was a long way to travel for cupcakes. Faith Schwartz's were the best around, but they were considered specialty items, not something the Amish would ordinarily buy for a child's birthday.

"I see," he said noncommittally.

"So the *Englischer* is leaving Willow Creek soon, *jah*?"

Through clenched teeth, Seth replied, "As you know, her name is Trina, but *jah*, she's moving the Sunday after this one, on May first."

"Who will care for the *buwe* until school lets out?" Fannie asked.

Seth didn't know why it was any of Fannie's business, but he was too tired to point that out to her. "I don't know," he said with a heavy sigh. "I thought I'd ask Emma Lamp."

"Emma Lamp? You haven't heard?"

"Heard what?"

"She broke her ankle chasing that scamp brother of hers, Thomas."

Seth tried not to show the disappointment he

felt. "I guess I'll have to make other arrangements." But who would he ask? Pearl and Ruth couldn't keep up with the boys. Iris might be able to, but she was already occupied tending to Ruth.

"I suppose I could help," Fannie volunteered, "since my sister-in-law lives right next door to me and her *kinner* are in school, too, I could take the *meed* to her house in the morning and pick them up when I return from your house toward evening."

I suppose now that Trina is leaving, Fannie isn't avoiding me any longer, Seth thought. As unpalatable as the idea of having her as a nanny was, he didn't have any other options. It would only be for a few weeks until school let out. As long as Fannie understood he wasn't interested in any other kind of relationship with her, he decided to accept her offer.

"I'd appreciate it," he said. Then, to emphasize it was an employment arrangement, he added, "I'll pay a fair wage, especially considering you'll have to *kumme* from Elmsville."

"*Gut*. I'll see you bright and early on Monday, May second. *Mach's gut*, Seth."

After she exited the shop, Seth shook his head. He knew he should have been grateful the Lord had provided him a solution to his problem, but all he could think about was that when Trina first arrived, he'd wished time would pass quickly until she left. Now he wished it would stand still.

Chapter Nine

While the boys were napping, Trina brought cups of tea into the parlor for herself and Martha. Ethan had arrived that morning before he headed to his office and looked Martha over. He'd said she seemed fine, but if she developed pain anywhere, she'd need to get X-rays. Apparently people didn't always realize how they landed when they fell and sometimes they broke their bones without knowing it.

Before leaving, he urged Martha to reconsider visiting an ophthalmologist. "It could change the quality of your life. Wouldn't you prefer to be more independent than you are now?"

Martha pretended her hearing was as poor as her vision and she didn't respond to his question, but Trina wanted to get to the bottom of the matter and find out why she refused to consider surgery. She also wanted to talk to Martha about the letter from Abe.

After taking a seat across from the older woman, Trina decided an indirect approach was best. "Martha," she started, "there's something I'd like to ask about Willow Creek's Amish *leit*. Does the *Ordnung* here prohibit modern *Englisch* medication and technology?"

"In other words, you want to know why I'm refusing to have eye surgery," Martha replied bluntly. Subtlety was lost on her. She explained, "I had an emergency removal of my gall bladder when I was in my fifties. The doctors botched the procedure and I needed a second surgery. I was in the hospital for a week. So, plain and simple, I'm scared to death of hospitals."

"Really?" Trina was stunned. She didn't think there was anything Martha was frightened of. "Is Seth afraid, too? He seems as reluctant to consult a medical doctor as you are."

"*Neh*. His aversion comes from something else… I told you how his brother left the Amish to marry an *Englischer*? Well, she was a nurse. Ever since then, Seth hasn't wanted to go anywhere near the hospital. He's afraid he'll bump into Kristine's old friends and seeing them will stir up memories he'd rather let rest. I think he's also developed a bias toward medical personnel. Seth doesn't trust them because he felt Kristine fooled him. He says if they'd deceive people in their personal lives, they'd lie to patients in their professional lives, too."

"That's *lecherich*—" Trina protested.

"*Jah*, it is. But it's probably ridiculous for me to be afraid, too, just because I had one bad operation when I was younger. Our perceptions and fears shape our truths and they shouldn't, because often they're wrong."

"You're right about that," Trina agreed. Then she delved into how she'd found the letter from her grandfather and what he'd written about her mother wanting to come back. "All this time I thought my *mamm* resented living in Willow Creek. I never knew she wanted to return. Every time I asked her about it, she said we were better off in the *Englisch* world."

"She was probably protecting you from knowing how much she wanted to return because she knew it wasn't a possibility. She didn't want you to feel sad on her behalf."

Trina's eyes overflowed. She'd ended up feeling sad on her mother's behalf anyway.

"Would you ever think about staying in Willow Creek?" Martha asked quietly.

"I've considered it," Trina replied as she dabbed her cheeks with a tissue. "But I don't know what I'd do for a living around here."

"The schoolteacher, Katie Yoder, is resigning at the end of the school year. I probably shouldn't mention this, but she's going to have a *bobbel* soon."

Trina's mood brightened. "Would the school board accept an *Englisch* schoolteacher?"

"They've done it in the past. Of course, they'd give preference to an Amish teacher."

Trina was afraid to voice the question she'd mulled over and prayed about all night, for fear of the answer. "Do you think…do you think there's any possibility I might become Amish?"

Martha pushed the rocker back and forth a few times before answering. "Ordinarily, I'd be doubtful. Most *Englischers* can't adjust to our lifestyle. There are too many obstacles in the way. The language, for one. Giving up modern conveniences, for another. And many of them are drawn to the lifestyle but they don't accept the faith that's at the core of everything we do."

Trina waited with bated breath to hear what Martha would say next.

"But given your background, as well as your faith and your demonstrated ability to forfeit modern conveniences, I think there's a *gut* likelihood the bishop would allow it, through conversion and convincement…if it's what you really want. But do you understand you'd be making the change for yourself and for the Lord, not for anyone else?"

Trina exhaled loudly. Now that the possibility was open to her, she knew it was exactly what she wanted. And she didn't want to become Amish simply because her mother had wanted it for her, nor because she was in love with Seth—although both had influenced her decision. Trina wanted it for herself. "I do," she said, as solemnly as if she were taking a wedding vow.

Martha was radiant. "Then we'll make an appointment to meet with the deacons and the bishop. You'll need an Amish woman to take you under her wing—I'll volunteer, if you agree."

"Of course I agree! I'd be so grateful," Trina said. From what she could tell, Martha had been mentoring her since she arrived. She asked the older woman not to tell Seth yet. Trina wanted to deliver the news herself for the pleasure of seeing his initial response in person.

"I won't say a word. Now, don't you think this calls for a celebratory funny cake?"

Trina laughed. Her days of feeling like a funny cake herself—unsure of whether she wanted to be Amish or *Englisch*—had come to a close. She had no question what she wanted to be. "I think you should teach me a new Amish recipe. I'm ready to try custard pie now."

The two women spent the rest of the afternoon baking. It was raining again so the boys were stuck inside but Trina was so elated she didn't even mind playing Noah's Ark another time. She positioned herself so she could see the lane, and when Seth's buggy appeared she ran outside without an umbrella to tell him about her decision.

"What's wrong? Is it my *Groossmammi*?" he asked when she burst into the stable—a place she'd tried to avoid because she was skittish around the livestock.

"*Neh*. Ethan said she checked out just fine," she quickly assured him. "Please, *kumme* closer to the door so I can see your face in the light. I have something *wunderbaar* to tell you."

Seth took a few steps closer. His hat was dripping so he removed it with one hand and raked his fingers through his hair with the other. He looked so handsome Trina almost forgot to speak and then the words rushed out. She told him about the letter and how she'd spoken to Martha and that she was going to stay in Willow Creek and join the Amish for good.

At first, Seth's expression was serious and

Trina knew he was taking it all in. But instead of growing happier, it seemed he grew graver, not uttering a word. When she finished speaking, he walked a few paces toward a post, then turned around and looked at her. Then he crossed to the other side of the stable and leaned against the opposite post, staring down at the hay strewn across the floor as if it were the most fascinating thing he'd ever seen.

She was on the brink of tears. "Aren't you going to say something?"

He slowly looked at her and asked, "What is it you want to hear, Trina?"

"I want to hear how you feel," she said, but suddenly, she wasn't so sure she did.

Seth's heart was making a racket in his ears. How he felt? On one hand, he was thrilled because this was too good to be true. And on the other hand—well, he was dubious because this was too good to be true. So which feeling should he tell her about?

"I'm surprised. I'm—I'm shocked, really..." he stammered.

Trina's chin was quivering. "That's it? That's your response?"

"How do you expect me to respond?" Seth snapped. Thunder rumbled in the distance; a spring storm was approaching.

"I don't know." Trina's beautiful voice had gone monotone. "Forget I asked."

"Wait." He pulled her arm and she stopped but wouldn't face him. He looked at the delicate swirl of her ear as he spoke. She might not be happy with what he was about to say but she deserved his honesty. "I'm apprehensive, Trina. I guess I'm—I'm afraid."

"Afraid?" Trina repeated. "You're *afraid*? Of what?"

Seth walked to a bale of hay and sat down. "I'm terrified I might believe you. Terrified you'll change your mind. Terrified of what that would do to the *buwe* and Martha." Choking, he added, "And to me. I've been down this road before. I've seen what it can do to a family…"

"Oh, Seth," Trina said and sat down next to him, their knees separated by the thinnest slice of space. "I'm not like Kristine. I won't change my mind. I want this more than anything. And I—wait, I'm probably saying the exact things she said, right?"

Seth nodded miserably. Kristine *had* said the same things. Over and over again. But in the end, she still changed her mind.

"I understand why you'd have your doubts. If I were in your shoes, I probably would, too," Trina said. "So I won't ask you to trust me. Instead, I'll keep showing you—and all the *leit* in Willow Creek—that I *am* trustworthy. I *am* true to my word. Time will prove it. You'll see."

Seth's heart ballooned because Trina was so understanding about the source of his disbelief. The truth was, he *wanted* to trust her and at least that was a strong step in the right direction. He turned his face toward hers and took in her earnest eyes and winsome expression. He wished he could allow himself one kiss on those lips, which he imagined would feel as velvety soft as the petals of a rose. Just one kiss before he said what he had to say, because once he said it, he couldn't take it back.

"You have to understand," he carefully began. He didn't want to sound presumptuous, but he needed her to know where he stood. "Even though your intention is to become Amish, until you've actually been baptized into the church, you're still *Englisch*."

"I understand," she whispered, tilting her chin toward him. Their mouths were even closer now and he looked at her from beneath lowered eyelids as he spoke.

"Which means an Amish man in Willow Creek wouldn't be allowed to court you. He wouldn't be able to kiss you." Seth's mouth felt parched and he had to lick his lips before continuing. "He wouldn't be allowed to tell you he loved you, no matter how much he wanted to."

"I understand. And I would respect him for that, no matter how much I wanted all those things, too," Trina stated seriously. "I would expect him to stay true to his beliefs and I wouldn't tempt him to violate them in any way." As if to prove it, Trina pulled her head back, stood up and walked toward the door.

Come back. Come closer, Seth thought, contradicting the very words he'd just spoken. But by moving away from him, Trina was demonstrating the sincerity of her intention to follow Amish practices and he loved her even more for that.

A sheet of rain fell outside the door but instead of exiting, Trina pivoted and said, "You know, Seth, I'm afraid, too. I'm afraid now that I've admitted how much I want this, I'm going to be turned down by the bishop. Martha said most people aren't successful at converting."

Seth had little fear of that and he said so. "You're not most people, Trina. You're different. You're the most unique *Englischer* I've ever met. And I'll support you through the convincement process however I can."

"Denki," Trina said, her skin aglow. "Now all I have to do is tell the realtor I've changed my mind about selling the house."

"You'll eventually have to get over your fear of barn animals, too," Seth joked.

Trina giggled. "I've conquered my fear of *hinkel*. Next, my fear of mice. Eventually I'll work my way up to horses and cows."

"It won't be easy," Seth said, and suddenly he wasn't joking anymore. "Not any of it." He was referring to himself waiting to see if she was really going to stay.

"But it will be worth it. You'll see," Trina said, again erasing his fears.

"Oh, *neh*!" Seth smacked his palm against his forehead. "I just remembered. Today I made arrangements for Fannie to watch the *kinner* starting on May second until school lets out."

Trina put her hands on her hips. "Fannie? That's who you chose to replace me?"

"I didn't want to, but there wasn't anyone else. I was worried about my *groossmammi*."

"Perhaps it's for the best. Martha agreed to mentor me, so now we can spend time alone together without waiting for the *buwe* to take their naps. Fannie will keep them occupied."

"More likely *they'll* keep *her* frustrated."

Trina giggled. "As long as no one winds up in the creek, I think you should be grateful."

Seth laughed. He reveled in their rapport; at least he wouldn't have to refrain from talking to her until she was baptized into the Amish church. Trina excitedly told him Martha was going to help her refine her *Deitsch,* sew an Amish wardrobe and learn to cook more Amish meals.

"Can I make a suggestion?" Seth asked and when Trina said yes, he continued, "Forget about refining your *Deitsch.* Instead, ask her to give you additional bread-making lessons. The loaves you make are like leather."

Now Trina cracked up. "*Jah*, but you love leather."

"I enjoy working with it, not chawing it."

"You'd make a terrible lion," she jested and they darted through the rain toward the house. Once he followed Trina inside, Seth shook his hair like a dog all over Timothy and Tanner, who were waiting for them at the door. They screeched with hilarity at his antics.

"It smells like custard pie in here," Seth noticed immediately. "If dessert smells this *appenditlich*, I can't imagine what we're having for supper."

"Actually, I haven't put supper together yet," Trina confessed. "Martha and I were so focused on baking the pie and talking about—"

"That's okay," Seth interjected. "I'm treating all of us to supper at Browns' Diner on

Main Street. *Buwe*, go tell *Groossmammi*," he instructed and the boys raced down the hall.

"Are you sure?" Trina asked coyly. "Browns' Diner is *Englisch*, isn't it?"

"*Jah,* but there's no rule against eating there and tonight is a special occasion," Seth said, winking at her. "Besides, since you're not returning to Philadelphia, you'd better get used to our local version of a Philly cheese-steak sandwich."

"That's probably the only thing I'm going to miss about Philadelphia," she said. Everything else about living there pales in comparison to my life in Willow Creek."

Seth knew exactly what she meant because he felt like every other woman paled in comparison to Trina.

Dianne Barrett was very understanding about Trina changing her mind. In fact, the realtor said she'd been hoping Trina would reconsider, since a quick sale wouldn't work in Trina's favor, given how much property she owned. To add to Trina's joy, Martha arranged to have the bishop and one of the deacons call on them a few days later on the Sabbath, since it was an off Sunday. While Seth discreetly disappeared with the boys to the creek, Trina and Martha discussed Trina's conversion with the two clergymen, who gave tentative approval of her efforts to begin the convincement process. There would be many formal requirements for her to meet before she was accepted into the church, but the deacon said he'd announce her intention the following Sunday, May first, when the *leit* gathered again for church.

Trina sailed through the week, as well as the following weekend. On Monday, May second, the lawyer visited her and finalized the paperwork for her to take ownership of her grandfather's house, just as they'd arranged from the beginning. Since it was Fannie's first day watching the *buwe*, Trina was free to meet with the attorney alone at home.

"Congratulations," he said, handing her the deed. "The house is yours to sell."

"I'm not selling. I'm staying," Trina replied with a huge grin on her face.

That evening, right after she spied Fannie's buggy heading back down the lane, Trina hurried next door to tell Martha and Seth it was official: she owned the house. The boys greeted Trina from where they were stomping in puddles in the lane. Seth must have permitted them to engage in their favorite activity in order to burn off a little energy before bedtime.

"Trina, *Groossmammi* said she's going to

your house tomorrow by herself. Why can't we *kumme*, too?" Tanner questioned.

"Fannie said we're not allowed," Timothy told him. "Remember? She said Trina might be able to wash *Daed*'s brain but she wasn't going to let her wash our brains."

"Is that true?" Tanner asked Trina. "I don't think I want my brain washed."

Trina was appalled. Had Timothy not heard right or did Fannie really say that? Because Seth didn't want the boys to accidentally tell other people about Trina's intention to convert, she'd agreed not to let Timothy and Tanner know until it had been announced in church on Sunday. Although Trina hadn't been able to attend the service, Seth informed her on Sunday evening the boys hadn't been present when the announcement was made. He suggested he'd sit down with Timothy and Tanner to talk about it when he had time to explain it thoroughly and answer any questions they had. Meanwhile, apparently word had spread to Fannie's district within hours.

"I think Fannie heard wrong because I'm not washing anyone's brains, I promise," Trina assured Tanner. "And if your *groossmammi* says you may *kumme* to my house with her tomorrow, then you may. I'll go talk to her about it now."

The boys whooped and resumed puddle jumping as Trina knocked on the kitchen door. There was no answer but Seth approached from the stable and warned the boys they had five more minutes to play. He let Trina inside, telling her Martha was resting because her head hurt.

"Because of her eyes again?"

"Maybe. Or maybe it was because of the kind of day she had."

Trina thought the latter was more likely the cause. Seeing dirty dishes piled in the sink, Trina felt a twinge of complacency knowing Fannie wasn't able to manage the household as well as Trina had. "I'm here to tell you and Martha it's official—the house is mine!" she exclaimed.

"That's *wunderbaar*," Seth said. "You made it two months. Now let's see if you can make it two years."

His comment reminded Trina of when she first met him and she wasn't sure if he was teasing or not, but she shrugged it off, retorting, "From the looks of it, you should be more worried about if your new nanny can make it here two *days*." Then she told him about Fannie's remark and asked when he was going to tell Timothy and Tanner that Trina was staying.

Seth hesitated, and this time Trina was insulted. She knew he still didn't fully believe she was here for good. It pained her, but considering all he'd been through with Freeman and Kristine, she understood. "Seth, I know it's difficult for you to believe, but I assure you I've already put every last *Englisch* thing out of my life. I even donated my *Englisch* Bible to my church. I'll use my *groossdaadi*'s German one, instead. From this moment forward, I'm going to live as an Amish person would, except when taking liberties would be inappropriate."

Seth remained silent so she continued. "If you don't want to tell the *buwe* yet, I understand and I'll respect that. But since the rest of the community found out during church yesterday, eventually the boys will, too. We have to tell them something, otherwise they'll be confused that I'm still here. And I don't want Fannie's explanations to take root in their minds."

Seth noncommittally offered, "Maybe I'll tell them tonight before putting them to bed."

"Oh, okay." Once again, Trina was disappointed by his reluctance, but she reminded herself she'd committed to showing him, however long it took, that she would honor her word.

The next day at five in the morning she woke

to rapid knocking and she sat up straight, panicking. Had Martha's headache worsened?

"What's the matter?" she asked Seth at the door as the *buwe* cavorted behind him.

"Nothing. It's time for milking. If you're serious about living like the Amish, you need to learn how to milk a cow. No more milk from a plastic jug."

Was he challenging her or trying to be helpful? Trina couldn't decide, but either way, she was willing to learn. "Great. Maybe later in the week you'll teach me to hitch the horse, too."

Even in the dreary early morning light, Trina caught his sparkling smile. "You were going to take it slowly," he reminded her. Then, as the boys ran to the stable ahead of them, Seth explained, "They were so excited to find out you're staying here they woke up before I did."

Seth must have told them the previous night! Trina was so delighted she nearly skipped to the barn like a child herself. After Seth gave her a preliminary demonstration of how to milk the cow, she returned home to make breakfast. While she was eating, Seth knocked on her door yet again, informing her Martha wouldn't be coming that day. Her head still hurt.

Although she was disappointed, Trina decided to give her home a more thorough spring cleaning than she had before Dianne visited. Now that the house was hers, she realized she couldn't keep Abe's door shut forever. She'd probably want to host overnight guests eventually, so she stood in the doorway trying to decide how to brighten the room yet keep the furnishings modest and plain, in accordance with the *Ordnung*. That's when she remembered she still hadn't looked at the letters and photos in Abe's nightstand, so she pulled open the drawer and removed the folder.

Sure enough, it contained a letter and photo for each year from the time Trina was born until she turned eighteen. She couldn't bear to read the letters in which her mother asked Abe if she could return, but flipping through the photos was like seeing a movie of her life. In one picture, she was crawling. In another, she was smiling broadly, showing off the gap where her tooth had fallen out. There was a photo of her riding a bicycle and another one of her standing primly in a new dress beneath a blossoming dogwood tree at Easter time. Filled with a mix of nostalgia and loneliness for her mother, Trina slid the items back into the folder. Since photographs weren't permitted, she'd have to get rid of them and rely on the images she knew by heart, instead.

Just then, something buzzed loudly in the

room. At first she thought a fat housefly had gotten into the house, but then she realized it was her cell phone, still sitting on the window-sill. The last time she'd used it was to finalize a meeting time with Dianne—or was it when she entered Ethan's phone number into it after finding the business card he'd left behind? In any case, she'd forgotten all about it. Making a mental note to cancel her service before discarding the phone, she briefly glanced at the screen and noted a text. It said:

It's me, your father. I'm about to call you. Please pick up. It's urgent.

She had just finished reading the text when the phone vibrated in her hand again. Fearful something was wrong, she felt compelled to answer her father's call.

"It's Trina," she said into the receiving end of the phone.

"Hello, Trina. Thank you for answering. I'm here in town and I need to talk to you. Will you meet with me? I'll pick you up and take you to lunch."

Her father was in Willow Creek? Trina was silent, her mind reeling.

"Trina, please. You're the only child I have. I don't want anything to come between us. I know I haven't been in touch, but I'd like to change that now."

Trina thought of how her mother had never gotten to reconcile with Abe. She didn't want that to happen with her father, too, especially since her mother had urged her not to turn him away if he wanted a relationship. Trina knew she had to listen to what her father had to say and to forgive him if he asked. She wanted to tell him about her choice to become Amish, too.

That's when she had an idea; she'd give the photos to her father, since he'd missed seeing Trina during so many of the years her mother had caught on camera. He'd probably be as delighted to get them as Abe had been. Trina separated them from the letters and took the folder with her to her room, where she changed into a fresh top and skirt, and then went out onto the porch to wait for her father there.

To her surprise, not one but two cars were already parked in the lane by her house. Because it was drizzling, she slipped the folder inside her coat so it wouldn't get wet and then sprang across the lawn and found both vehicles were empty. Twirling around to scan the yard, Trina spotted two men walking up from the creek. She didn't know one of them, but the other one was definitely her father. Although

Trina hadn't seen him in years, she'd recognize him anywhere, even though he was balding now and had developed a bit of a paunch.

When he came near, he kissed her cheek and said, "You look exactly like your mother did at your age. Beautiful." After a pause, he added, "I'm sorry she's gone, Trina."

He really did look sorry, too, and Trina felt a pang of guilt for being so resentful she couldn't locate him in time for her mother's funeral. She extended her hand to the short, dark-haired man accompanying her father and said, "I'm Trina."

"Oh, sorry," Richard apologized. "Trina, this is my business associate, Drex Watson—"

It suddenly dawned on Trina what her father and this man were doing down by the creek; they'd been scoping out the property. Drex was probably there to help persuade—no, to *pressure*—Trina to reconsider selling the land to her father. Trina's temper flared and she didn't give her father a chance to finish making introductions. "I've already told the realtor I have no intention of selling the property for development purposes. So there's no need for you to accompany us, Mr. Watson." She deliberately used a formal address to indicate they weren't on friendly terms.

"Trina, wait. Just consider—" Drex began to protest, but Trina's father interrupted him.

"It's okay, Drex. My daughter wants to speak with me alone. I'll catch up with you later."

Drex's eyes darted from Richard to Trina and then back to Richard before he shrugged and said, "Alright. Catch you later."

After Drex drove away, Richard said, "Come on, Trina, it's raining. Let's go get some lunch in town, okay?"

Trina hesitated. On one hand, she wanted to hear him out. On the other hand, she didn't want him pressuring her to change her mind about selling to him. She slowly walked to the car and accompanied him to Browns' Diner. As they drove, Trina realized his vehicle was worth a fortune and she wondered if Kurt had been exaggerating how broke her father actually was.

At the diner Richard chose a booth by the front window and while they waited for their meals, Trina told him about her decision to become Amish. He looked surprised but didn't say anything as she described the process she'd undergo before being baptized into the church.

When she was done speaking, her father said, "So, while you're going through this—

what did you call it, convincement process?—you'll live with your mentor?"

Trina cocked her head. "No. I'll live in my own house. Why?"

Her father's cheeks broke out in ruddy patches. "I just wondered, that's all."

"Dad," Trina said firmly, although the term felt strange to her ears, "I'm *not* going to sell the house. To anyone."

"I understand," he said, but his mouth sagged. Trina waited for him to change the subject—specifically, to talk about his desire to reconcile with her, but he stayed silent until the server brought them their meals. By that time, Trina had realized he never truly intended to come back into her life, except to purchase her house. She poked at her fries but didn't take a bite since she wouldn't have been able to swallow.

After her father paid the check, Trina summoned the last of her grace and reached over to clasp his hand. "Dad, even though I'm becoming Amish, I'll always welcome you into my home as a guest," she said. "And I'll always welcome you into my life as my father."

He glanced up. *Green eyes. Is that all we have in common?* Trina wondered as she waited for him to speak, but he didn't say a word. Then the server returned with his change and her father pulled his hand out from under Trina's to pocket the bills.

Trina decided she'd walk home and her father didn't object even though it was raining harder now. Before she stood to leave she remembered the folder of photos and she pushed it across the table toward him. "I want you to have these memories from my childhood. Even though it was difficult sometimes and I wished you were with us, Mom and I were happy together." Rising, she leaned over the table to kiss his head before saying, "Take care, Dad."

Then she stepped outside, where raindrops and teardrops rolled steadily down her face.

Shortly before Seth was going to leave for the day, Joseph Schrock stopped in to report the south end of Willow Creek was blocked off because the creek had overflowed its banks and Meadow Road was submerged.

"I'll walk home on West Street, instead," Seth said. "*Denki* for telling me. Otherwise I would have had to double back once I got to Meadow Road."

"I only found out myself when I returned from an appointment in Highland Springs this afternoon. Otherwise, I would have warned Trina, too. Poor *maedel,* it must have taken her over an hour to get home from the diner."

"Trina was in the diner?" Seth wondered why she had ventured out in the inclement weather.

"*Jah*, I saw her eating with an *Englischer*. He looked old enough to be her *daed*. Anyway, *mach's gut*, Seth." Joseph gave a brief wave of his hand and slipped back out the door.

As Seth trudged home, he was so consumed with wondering who Trina met at the diner he didn't notice the rain had soaked through his coat to his shirt until he arrived at the house and Fannie handed him a towel.

"Where's my *groossmammi*?" he asked, patting his sleeves dry.

"She's in her room with the door closed. I think her *koppweh* might have gotten worse. Probably from the *buwe*—they've been very loud today."

"And where are they?"

"In the basement. I'll start to make supper now that you're home."

The last thing Seth wanted was for Fannie to stay any longer. "That's alright. I'm sure your daughters are waiting to see you. We'll just have sandwiches."

Fannie's shoulders drooped in disappointment, so Seth quickly offered, "I'll hitch your buggy for you and bring it around so you won't get wet."

"*Denki.* I'd appreciate that," she replied. Ever so casually, she added, "Unlike Trina and her two *Englisch* guests, I have no interest in strolling around in the rain."

Seth couldn't help taking her bait. "Trina had guests today?"

"*Jah.* She was walking around her yard with two men. It seemed as if they were surveying the property."

Seth's stomach lurched as he briefly wondered if Trina was reconsidering selling. He just as quickly dismissed the notion. Trina would never do that. But why was she showing anyone the property, especially in the rain? Seth could hardly wait for the boys to go to sleep so he could go talk to her. First, he checked on Martha, who refused anything to eat, and then he made sandwiches for the boys, gave them baths and tucked them into bed.

"Is everything okay?" Trina asked as she let him in.

"I don't know. Maybe you'd like to tell me," he said, crossing the threshold.

"What do you mean?" Her face was puckered with confusion.

He wasn't in the mood for their usual repartee. "Don't play games, Trina."

"What are you talking about, Seth?" Now her hands were on her hips. "And why do I suspect Fannie is at the bottom of whatever's troubling you?"

"Maybe it's because you know she knows you had men here looking at your property."

"Oh, that." The scowl faded from Trina's face as she sat down at the table, waving her hand dismissively. How could she be so casual? "*Jah*, my *daed* and his business associate came here and, *jah*, they were looking at the land. But I made it clear to them I wasn't interested in selling."

"Was this before or after you ate lunch with them in the diner?"

Trina's head jerked back. "Wow. I know Willow Creek is a small community, but I didn't realize just how many people are interested in my business."

"So it's true, you had dinner with them?"

"Not with *them*. I ate dinner with my *daed*. Alone. Is that a crime?"

"Was it your idea?" Seth was annoyed he had to grill her for details. If she had nothing to hide, why wasn't she being more forthcoming?

"I don't know why that matters, but *neh*, he was the one who texted me. He wanted to get together and I felt I owed him that much. I wanted to tell him I'd always—"

"He *texted* you? You still have your cell phone?" Seth was astounded.

"*Jah*. I'd forgotten all about it until I heard the text notification go off."

Seth paced the length of the kitchen. This was exactly how things had started to unravel with Kristine's plans to join the Amish. First, it was her cell phone she couldn't give up. Then it was her favorite pieces of jewelry. Next, it was her laptop. She always had a compelling excuse for keeping whatever it was she wanted to keep—including Freeman. Now here was Trina, making similar excuses just one day after she promised him she'd put every last *Englisch* thing out of her life. Worse, it was just one day after he'd told his young, vulnerable sons about her plan to convert! Seth was seething.

"Your cell phone. Your father. Your father's business associate." He counted on his fingers, listing her offenses. "What other parts of your *Englisch* life are you still holding on to?"

"Are you kidding me?" Trina asked with knives in her voice. "After everything I've given up, do you really believe there's any aspect of *Englisch* life I'm deliberately hanging on to?"

"Clearly there is," Seth barked. His volume rose as he continued, "I just wish you would have recognized you weren't fully committed to leaving your *Englisch* life behind before I told the *buwe* you were converting. It will devastate them if you change your mind."

"You know I understand that better than anyone!" Trina countered, her nostrils flaring. "I'd never break such an important promise to Timothy and Tanner because I remember exactly how destructive it was when my *daed* didn't keep his promises to me."

"That's exactly what I'm worried about." Seth glowered back at her. "Maybe it's like *daed*, like *dochder*. Can't trust him, can't trust you."

Trina slapped her palms against the table and jumped to her feet, leaning forward to glare directly into his eyes. "The problem isn't that I'm untrustworthy—it's that *you're* untrusting. So if you want to live the rest of your life distrustful and afraid, go right ahead. But you're not the only one who's going to miss out—your attitude is going to harm your *buwe*, too. And that's as unfair to them as my *daed* was to me."

She twirled and stormed out of the room at the same time Seth stomped outside into the rain. As angry as Trina was, he was twice as livid. He didn't regret it one iota that he'd challenged her commitment. No matter what she said about his so-called distrustful attitude affecting Timothy and Tanner, if there was even an inkling of doubt Trina wasn't going to stay, it was Seth's parental duty to protect his sons from becoming even more attached to her. He resolved from then on to keep them away from her—and to keep himself away from her, too.

Chapter Ten

Trina waited until she was sure Seth had left before she emerged from her room, slamming the door behind her. Who did he think he was, acting as if she'd committed a crime by meeting with her father? And who did he think *she* was to suggest she didn't want to let go of her *Englisch* life? She circled the parlor, ranting aloud, "If I wanted to hold on to my *Englisch* life, I wouldn't have forfeited a half a million dollar sale in order to stay here!"

Her anger gave her a surge of energy. She pulled a sack of flour from the pantry and yeast from the fridge and began making bread. Nothing ever felt as good as kneading the dough hard and punching it down. She made four loaves in succession while flashes of lightning illuminated the sky and thunder raged outside as tempestuously as she did.

She realized she was sick and tired of trying to prove herself to Seth. She was almost grateful he'd said such awful things because it showed her he wasn't going to change. What good would it do for him to trust her after she'd become Amish? That wasn't trust; that was proof. She wanted him to trust her now, before she converted. She wanted him to have faith in the best, not to always suspect the worst.

And what about *him* keeping *his* word? He'd said he'd support her however he could during her convincement process. What hypocrisy! He accused *her* of being like her father, but he was more like Richard Smith than she'd ever be. She was crushed to discover he was like every man who'd ever left her when she most needed help, and suddenly her anger completely fizzled out, leaving her feeling dejected and alone. Desperate for consolation, she read and reread the letters her mother sent Abe until the accounts of happier times soothed her heartache enough that she could finally go to sleep.

The next day, when Timothy and Tanner knocked on the door, Trina pushed her lips into a smile to conceal the sadness that had returned. "Hello, *buwe*. Did you *kumme* over here alone?"

"*Jah*. Fannie said we had to scamper quickly. She's waiting over there." Timothy turned and pointed to Fannie, who was standing out of the rain beneath a willow in the Helmuths' yard. Why wasn't she accompanying the boys? Was she afraid she'd become tainted by visiting someone who was still an *Englischer*? Trina took a small measure of satisfaction in lifting her hand in a friendly wave, but Fannie just looked at her shoes.

"Would you like to *kumme* in?" she asked the boys. "I made sweet bread last night."

"*Neh*, *Daed* said we're not allowed," Tanner said. "But Fannie told us we have to visit you this one time."

Trina suppressed a gasp, outraged that Seth was using the boys to take out his anger at her. "Why did Fannie want you to *kumme* here?"

"We're supposed to tell you *Groossmammi* can't visit you today. Her head is splitting," Tanner reported.

"Oh, dear, do you mean she has a splitting *koppweh*?"

"*Jah*. And *Daed*'s getting a blue face."

"A what?" Trina didn't think she'd heard correctly.

Timothy said, "*Groossmammi* told *Daed* he could talk about it until his face turns blue but she wasn't changing her mind. And *Daed* said he wasn't changing his mind, either. He said he couldn't stop *Groossmammi* from visiting you but he could stop his *buwe* from visiting you."

"And *Groossmammi* cried and went to her room because of her head splitting," Tanner added. Scrunching his nose, he asked, "Will it hurt when *Daed*'s face turns blue?"

For the boys' sake, Trina fought to keep her ire at Seth in check. "I don't think your *daed*'s face is really going to turn blue," she explained carefully. "Sometimes people use funny words called idioms but the words aren't really what they mean. Like if I say yesterday it rained cats and dogs, there weren't really cats and dogs falling from the sky. I just mean it rained hard."

"Like when Fannie told *Daed* he was as strong as an ox she didn't mean it? Because an ox is really strong and *Daed* is really strong but *Daed* can't pull a plough."

It just figures Fannie would appeal to Seth's masculinity like that, Trina thought. To Tanner she said, "Exactly like that. So don't you worry about your *daed*. What you ought to do is be especially kind to your *groossmammi* today. Can you do that?"

"Jah," the boys readily agreed, as Trina knew they would. She ducked into the kitchen,

slipped two loaves of bread into separate bags and returned to hand one to each of them.

"Timothy can carry the cinnamon-raisin bread and, Tanner, you carry this sweet bread. If Fannie says it's okay, you may have a piece. And guess what? It's not even tough like carrion!"

Pleased she'd elicited a smile from the boys' serious faces, she kissed their heads and sent them off with a reminder to tell Martha she'd see her when she was feeling better. The boys darted back to Fannie, who was already walking toward the Helmuths' house.

Trina couldn't help worrying about Martha's health. Whether her headaches had increased because of her vision problem or because of her "nanny problem," it seemed she'd benefit from a visit to the doctor. *But if I suggest that again, Seth will just tell her it's because I haven't let go of my* Englisch *ways*, Trina thought bitterly.

Knowing she needed to improve her German comprehension as well as her attitude, Trina sat down, picked up her Bible and began reading until there was a break in the rain. Then she walked into town to do her shopping and inquire about summer employment. She had to take the long way, avoiding both Meadow Road and the path along the creek because of the flooding, but she felt so listless she didn't mind. After picking up her groceries, she stopped at Schrock's Shop to ask about a job.

Joseph told her he didn't have any openings right then, but in another month he might need extra help, since so many tourists came through town once school let out. Before Trina left he asked if Meadow Road was still flooded. When she confirmed it was, he sympathized because her section of Willow Creek was cut off to traffic on three sides. To Trina, it hardly mattered since she traveled by foot, not by buggy. Also, now there was less of a chance that her father would return. Not that she expected him to.

The sky began pouring again on her way home and she was drenched by the time she reached her door. She was bending to unlace her shoes when she thought she heard her name being called from a distance. She straightened her spine, listening.

"Trina!" That was definitely Tanner outside her door. She flung it open. His face was bright red and he was panting.

Crouching down, she placed her hands on his shoulders. "Take a deep breath and then tell me what happened."

"Timothy fell off his bicycle in the basement. He was going real fast around a corner and his bike tipped and he went flying through the air and he landed like this," Tanner said, gesturing with his hands. "Fannie is crying and *Groossmammi* wants you to *kumme*."

Although her heart was drumming in her ears, Trina had the presence of mind to grab her cell phone before she ran across the yard and into the house with Tanner. When they reached the bottom of the basement stairs, she found Martha and Fannie kneeling beside Timothy, who was lying on the floor, moaning. As Trina leaned closer, she noticed his arm was swollen and positioned oddly.

"It's broken—his arm is broken!" Fannie seemed nearly hysterical. "And he might have a concussion, too!"

Under her breath, Trina hissed, "Shh! Calm down and don't move him." If Timothy had a head or neck injury, Trina didn't want to splint his arm. She quietly asked Timothy if he'd hit his head, but he didn't answer, so she gingerly parted his blond curls to examine his skull. There was no blood, but a large egg was already forming on the right side.

She quickly pulled her phone out of her pocket. She'd gladly suffer any consequences or shaming remarks from Seth for using her cell phone: Timothy's health was more important to her than anything else at that moment. She tapped in 911.

When the operator came on the line, Trina described their emergency. The operator said they'd dispatch an ambulance, but it might take a while for it to get there because of the flooding. He asked if there was anyone nearby with a car who could reach them quicker and bring Timothy to the hospital. Trina said no before suddenly remembering Ethan. The dispatcher wanted to stay on the line with her, so after Trina gave him Ethan's number, he told another dispatcher to contact Ethan, who confirmed he'd be there as soon as possible. Once Martha heard help was on the way, she stopped ringing her hands and pressed them together, praying, "*Denki*, Lord!" and Trina inwardly echoed her gratitude to God.

She instructed, "Tanner, I'd like you to lead your *groossmammi* upstairs by the hand and let Dr. Gray in when he arrives. Fannie, bring me a quilt to keep Timothy warm." Fannie looked so peaked Trina was afraid she might pass out, so in what she hoped was a convincing voice she added, "Timothy's going to be okay, Fannie. Really, he will."

As the others clambered up the stairs, Trina cooed to the boy, "I know it hurts but you're doing great. Could you say your name so I know you're okay?" When he continued to moan without answering her, she asked, "What's the fiercest animal you can think of right now?"

"A shark," he mumbled, to her relief. In order to keep him awake and to prepare him for what would happen at the hospital, she told him a story about a shark that broke its fin. "The fish doctor said the shark needed to get an X-ray, which is what you'll probably get and it won't hurt at all. An X-ray is like a drawing of the bones on the inside of your skin."

Without opening his eyes, Timothy argued, "But sharks don't have bones. They have cartilage."

Trina could have wept for joy at his remark—clearly his brain was functioning just fine! A few minutes later Ethan arrived and evaluated Timothy's pupils, head, neck and spine, and then made a temporary splint to immobilize his arm and lifted him up.

"Instead of waiting for the ambulance, it'll be quicker for us to take him to the hospital. They'll need to set his arm, which might involve surgery, depending on the fracture. We'll have to take West Street to avoid the flooded areas. When we pass through town we can pick up Seth since we'll need his permission to treat Timothy."

When they got to Main Street, Ethan pulled over in front of Seth's shop and left the car running as he dashed into the store. A few moments later, three *Englisch* shoppers spilled onto on the sidewalk and Seth and Ethan followed closely behind.

Seth slid into the back seat with Trina and Timothy, careful not to jostle his son. "Please, *Gott*, ease Timothy's pain and keep him well," he prayed aloud. Timothy's eyes briefly fluttered open at the sound of Seth's voice before closing again.

Seeing Seth's affliction, Trina wanted to comfort him. No matter how angry she'd been, she wouldn't wish the kind of distress he was experiencing on anyone. But she was deeply shaken, too, and her addled mind couldn't come up with anything encouraging to say. She remained silent until Ethan pulled into the emergency entrance area. They were met by two staff members with a gurney who eased Timothy out of the back seat. Seth and Ethan followed them inside, while Trina drove the car to the parking lot, her hands trembling on the steering wheel.

Seth felt as if he had rocks in his gut as the hospital staff wheeled his son away. Before Ethan joined them, he assured Seth that Timothy would be in good hands. After filling out the necessary paperwork at the front desk, Seth paced the hallway, too distraught to sit with the others in the main waiting room. He silently pleaded with the Lord to keep close watch on Timothy. His prayers quickly turned into self-admonishment. How could he have been so irresponsible as to let Fannie watch the boys after what had happened the day she was alone with them by the creek?

Timothy's suffering was his fault and Seth wished he could take his son's place. For the first time in a long while, he thought of Eleanor. "I'm sorry," he whispered, leaning his head against the wall. All she had asked of him was, if he remarried, to choose a woman who would take good care of the boys. He hadn't even found a nanny who would take good care of them. Other than Trina, that was. "I'm so sorry," he whispered again.

A hand rested flat against his back. "Seth?" It was Trina and her hair was dripping wet. He'd been too distraught to notice if she'd been wet in the car on the way, but for a moment his mind flashed to the Sunday when he'd first courted Fannie and he'd picked Trina up on the roadside. He wished he could turn the clock back to that day. He would have trusted his initial perspective that he and Fannie weren't a match.

"Let's sit." Trina motioned to a backless wooden bench farther down the hall. "It's quieter there, so we can pray."

But Seth couldn't form any words, so Trina petitioned the Lord on his behalf. They sat with their heads bowed for what seemed like hours until finally Ethan came to tell them Timothy was going to be fine. He said the fracture was an ugly one but it didn't require surgery. However, the doctors wanted to keep him overnight because of the swelling. After it subsided, they'd cast his arm. The really great news was that he didn't appear to have a concussion.

"*Denki,* Lord! *Denki!*" Seth exclaimed, looking heavenward as a few tears streamed from his eyes down his cheeks and into his sideburns. "Is Timothy awake? May I see him?"

"He's groggy from the medication they gave him before setting the bone but you can go in," Ethan replied. "Sorry, Trina, it's family only until they transfer him to a room."

Whatever Trina might have said in reply, Seth didn't hear it. All he could focus on was seeing his son. Tears again sprang from his eyes when he viewed Timothy's small form reclining on the white bed. He hurried to his child's side and kissed the top of his head, but Timothy was too drowsy to stir. As the nurse was making arrangements to secure a room for him in the pediatric wing, Seth returned to the hall where Ethan and Trina had been.

Finding Ethan there alone, he asked, "Where's Trina?"

"She's driving back to your house to tell your *groossmammi* Timothy is going to be okay. Then she'll return with a few things for you, since she figured you'll probably want to stay overnight with him here. She'll pick me up then, too."

Seth felt horrible. After all of the cruel things he'd said to Trina, she was repaying him with kindness. Seth was indebted to Ethan, too. "I can't tell you how grateful I am for your medical expertise," he told him.

Ethan clasped his shoulder. "I'm blessed the Lord enabled me to study medicine and gave me an aptitude for it," he said. "But all of my knowledge wouldn't have done much good if Trina hadn't had the 911 dispatcher call me as soon as she did. If they had contacted me even ten minutes later, I wouldn't have made it to your house because my road was flooding over. I had to drive through about eight inches of standing water as it was."

It dawned on Seth that since the phone

shanty was on a road flooded by the creek, the only way Trina could have called 911 was by using her cell phone. He shuddered, thinking what could have happened. "She's been a blessing to my family in more ways than one," Seth told Ethan. Now he hoped he could find a way to express his appreciation to Trina— if she was even willing to talk to him. She'd been awfully quiet on the ride to the hospital, although Seth figured it was because she was worried about Timothy, too. He didn't think she could have been any more concerned if Timothy had been her own child.

By the time Trina returned to the hospital and located Seth in the pediatric wing, Ethan had gone to check on a patient who happened to have been admitted that day, too, and Seth was walking back to Timothy's new room after buying a coffee in the cafeteria.

Holding out a bag she said, "It's a change of clothes. And a sandwich for supper—Fannie made it."

"Denki," was all he could say even though he wanted to express so much more.

Averting her eyes, she asked how Timothy was and Seth grinned. Here was his chance. "He's terrific, thanks to you and Ethan. Ethan's visiting a patient, by the way. He said he'd be back soon. Listen, Trina, I—"

A nurse interrupted him as she exited Timothy's room. "Oh, there you are. Timothy's awake and he's asking for you. He won't believe me that you didn't leave. Could you please go show him you're still here, Mr. and Mrs. Helmuth?"

Glancing at Trina, who had brushed her hair into a bun and changed into a dry skirt and a plain, modest blouse, Seth understood why the nurse mistook her for an Amish woman. But he had a feeling Trina was insulted to be referred to as his wife.

"Of course," she replied to the nurse and Seth's hope surged. Maybe she wasn't as disgusted by his recent behavior as he feared. Then she added, "I can't wait to see him again," and Seth realized she was willing to overlook the nurse's error if it meant she had access to Timothy's room.

They found him sitting up in his bed that was fitted with sheets that had monkeys printed on them. Timothy greeted Trina before saying, "I was scared, *Daed.* I thought you left."

"*Neh*, I'd never leave, *suh*," Seth promised. The words seemed to catch in his throat. Hadn't Trina repeatedly offered Seth the same assurance? Realizing he'd been acting like a child himself, Seth almost wished Timothy would go back to sleep so he could apologize to Trina for his immature behavior, among other things.

"Timothy, did you paint those toucans on the walls?" she teased, pointing to the jungle motif wallpaper.

"Neh." Timothy's giggle was music to Seth's ears—just as Trina's voice had so often struck him as musical. "Dr. Levine said they have an acqua…an acquar…um, a home for real, live fish I can see in the common room tomorrow morning. Can Tanner *kumme* see it, too?"

"If your *daed* says it's okay, I think I can arrange a way to get Tanner and your *groossmammi* here," Trina said. Inwardly, Seth cringed, recognizing how careful Trina was being to defer all decisions regarding the children to him. It was as if she was a stranger, unsure of whether her help would be welcomed, and Seth knew he was the one who'd created that distance between them.

After a couple of minutes, Ethan knocked on the door and, seeing Trina, asked if she was ready to go. Seth wished he could steal a moment to speak with her in private, but before he could think of a way to take her aside, she gently kissed Timothy on his cheek and was gone.

Timothy soon dozed off again and slumbered peacefully through the night, but Seth didn't sleep a wink. As he watched his son's chest rise and fall, he recognized how blessed he was to have his family and he thanked God for them. He again thought about Trina using her cell phone to call the emergency service dispatcher and how relieved he was she hadn't gotten rid of it after all. He was just as grateful for Ethan's car, which delivered Timothy to the emergency room. And for the knowledge of the doctors and nurses who tended to him.

Ultimately, Seth knew it was the Lord who'd saved his son from worse harm, but He'd done it through Ethan, Trina and a handful of other *Englischers*. Of course, Seth had no intention of relying on *Englisch* transportation or technology for his daily needs, but he was ashamed when he recalled the insulting things he'd said to Trina about *Englishers* in general, and about her in particular. His desire to put things right between them consumed his thoughts and coursed through his body, almost like a physical pain, until the sun rose and Timothy finally awoke again.

Thrilled to have his breakfast in bed, Timothy refused any help from Seth and deftly fed himself using his left hand, which pleased the nurses and doctor. As Timothy was eating, Tanner and Martha walked into the room and Tanner's eyes lit up when he noticed the wallpaper. He carefully crawled atop the adjustable bed so Timothy could give him a "ride" on it, and while the boys played, Seth asked Martha how she got there.

"Fannie brought us. She's waiting in the buggy lot. I think she's afraid to *kumme* in."

"She should be!" Seth sputtered.

"Seth, you've been through a hard night." Martha pointed her index finger at him. "But this accident could have happened under anyone's care. It could have happened if you were with the boys, or if I was or if Trina was. Instead of casting blame, you ought to be grateful the Lord watched over Timothy as He did."

Seth swallowed. Martha was right, of course. "That's very true, *Groossmammi*. And I am grateful. Especially for Trina and Ethan. And for your prayers, too, because I know they were as vital to Timothy's well-being as the physical care he received here was." To keep himself from tearing up, Seth teased, "I have to admit, though, I'm surprised you wanted to come anywhere near a hospital."

"I could say the same to you!" Martha joked and they both cracked up. She continued, "Sometimes, our thoughts are irrational. They're based on fear, not truth. This hospital—these doctors—played a role in Timothy's healing, by *Gott*'s grace. It's not right for me to be so mistrustful of them because some other doctor made a mistake in my past."

Seth recognized Martha was no longer talking about hospitals, but about him and Trina—and Freeman and Kristine. "You're right again," he said, knuckling his eyelids.

"You ought to go home and get some sleep," Martha directed. "I think Fannie would appreciate knowing you aren't angry with her. Tanner and I will stay here and you can pick us up this afternoon. The nurse at the station said Timothy wouldn't be discharged until four or five."

Seth hesitated. "I don't want to leave Timothy. He's scheduled to get his cast on at two thirty."

"*Kumme* back by two, then," Martha said. "It's time to exercise a little trust, Seth. I'll be here and the doctors will take *gut* care of him if anything goes wrong. It won't, but the Lord never minds if we pray about things that trouble us."

On that note, Seth conceded. After bidding goodbye to the boys and assuring Timothy he'd return before he got his cast on, Seth headed to the special parking lot equipped with hitching posts for the area's Amish population.

When he climbed into the buggy, Fannie burst into tears. "I'm so sorry, Seth," she cried.

Seth repeated his grandmother's words. "It's alright. It's not your fault. Timothy's accident could have happened while anyone was watching him."

Fannie twisted to face him. "I know *that*," she said with a sniff. "What I'm sorry about is that I can't take care of the boys any longer. They're just too rambunctious."

Seth could barely respond he was so flabbergasted. "I understand," he uttered and neither of them said anything else all the way to his home.

As she drove up the lane, Fannie said, "In a way, it's a *gut* thing this happened. Not that Timothy's suffering is *gut*, but the entire incident showed me our families won't ever be compatible. I hoped once the *Englischer* wasn't watching your *kin* any longer they'd take a liking to me, and if we worked at it, eventually our families would grow to understand and cooperate with each other. But my *meed* and I are just too different from you and your *buwe*."

Seth simply nodded and thanked Fannie for bringing him home. He was so weary he went into the parlor and collapsed onto the sofa and covered his eyes with his hands. He'd made such a mess of things with Trina. Between that and all his pent-up tension over Timothy's accident, Seth had never felt so low, and he allowed himself to shed a few more tears before pulling out a handkerchief and blowing his nose.

Then he stood up. Before catching a nap, he needed to milk the cow, otherwise her udders would become too full and she'd run the risk of infection. He lumbered to the stable as if his feet were made of lead and pulled the door open, his eyes adjusting to the light. What he saw was so unexpected at first he thought he imagined it.

Trina glanced toward the stable door. She had intended to finish milking Bossy before Seth arrived, but she hadn't even started. Each time she held out an apple slice, trying to entice the cow to move toward the stanchion, Bossy lifted her head and stuck out her tongue to accept the treat. Trina was so afraid of being bitten she dropped the fruit on the ground. She was down to her last slice when Seth arrived.

Now that the worst of Timothy's crisis was over, all of the comments Seth made to Trina the previous day came rushing back and she was immediately on guard. Dropping the last piece of apple to the ground, she muttered defensively, "I guess this is one more thing *Englischers* aren't good at doing." She tossed her chin in the air and tried to flounce around him, but he stepped into her path, blocking her exit.

In her peripheral vision, she noted his nose and cheeks were red and raw, and his eyes were watery. He looked absolutely miserable.

"*Denki*, Trina," he said.

Without looking at him she shrugged and said, "As you can see, I couldn't even get her to *kumme* to the stanchion."

"Well, *denki* for trying. And *denki* for saving Timothy from further harm—" Seth's voice quivered and he swiped his hand across his eyes.

"I didn't save him. *Gott* did. All I did was make a phone call—on a cell phone," she pointed out.

"I'm so grateful you still had the phone."

Was that his idea of an apology? If he still thought she'd intentionally held onto the phone, his gratitude was meaningless. "I'm glad I had it, too, but I didn't keep it deliberately, no matter what you think."

"I believe you and I'm sorry I ever doubted you. And I don't know if you'll believe me, but I trust you more than anyone. I didn't realize just how much I trusted you until…until Timothy's accident. But I trust you with the most important thing in my life—my *kinner.* I trust you with my family, Trina."

Now Trina gazed into his eyes. Not so she could read his expression, but so he would have to read hers. "I trusted you with the most important thing in my life, too, Seth. I trusted you with my heart."

A tear escaped the corner of his eye and then another from his other eye. He pushed them away before soberly promising, "I know you did. And I'm so sorry I didn't care for your heart as lovingly as you cared for my family. I will do anything to make it right. Please give me another chance to prove *I'm* trustworthy, Trina. Please don't leave Willow Creek."

Despite the seriousness of the moment, Trina snorted. "Ha! Do you really think I'd give up my plan to become Amish because of you?"

Seth looked taken aback.

"I cared about you—I still care—more than any man I've ever known, Seth. But I wasn't becoming Amish because of you and I'm not going to leave the Amish because of you. I'm doing it because I think it's the best way for me to live out my faith."

Seth looked chagrined. "I don't know whether to feel humbled or insulted by that," he admitted, "but actually, I just feel happy because it means you're going to stay here."

"There's something else you need to know. I was saying goodbye to my father at the diner. But first I wanted him to know I wasn't holding a grudge and the door to a relationship with me would always be open. I didn't want to wait until it was too late, the way my *groossdaadi* waited until it was too late to restore his relationship with my *mamm*. He waited until it was too late to tell her he loved her."

His chin quivering noticeably, Seth asked, "If I told you now that I love you, would it be too late?"

Trina caught her breath, aching from the near promise in his words. "*If* you told me now, it wouldn't be too late—but it would be inappropriate. I'm not Amish. Not yet."

Seth's eyes shone a pure pale blue. "Then I guess I'll just have to wait until you are. And while I'm waiting, I'll try to become the kind of trustworthy man you can love, too."

To Seth's delight, Trina grinned mischievously and stuck her hand out to shake his. "Deal," she said.

Her skin was silky but her grasp was strong, just as on the first day he met her, when they were still strangers. "Stay right there," he said. "I have something for you."

He ran to his workshop behind the barn and returned with the picture frame, which he had wrapped in brown paper. After opening it, she sighed as she traced the etched sandpipers with her finger.

"It's to replace the one I broke," he said nervously, unsure of what she was thinking.

"It's beautiful. So beautiful," she murmured and hugged it to her chest. Then she looked at it again and sighed, "But photographs are forbidden."

"I think in this case, it's probably alright if you save the photo of you and your mother, as long as it's not prominently displayed in your parlor or anything."

"But, Seth, I gave that picture to my *daed* yesterday, along with the photos from Abe."

"You did?" Seth was amazed and crushed at the same time. The very day he'd accused Trina of holding on to her *Englisch* life, she had already given up the most precious *Englisch* possession she owned.

"But maybe I can use it to frame a certificate listing the years of my mother's birth and her passing?"

Displaying such certificates was an acceptable practice in the Amish community and Seth agreed, although he felt disappointed, too. "That's a *gut* idea, but I really wanted to give you a special place to store your treasured photo."

"I know you did and I appreciate it. But I'm already storing the image in a special place," she said, placing her hand over her heart. "It's right here, next to the love I have for other cherished people in my life."

Seth nodded. She didn't have to say anything more. He knew what she meant because he felt exactly the same way.

"I'd better start the milking," he said. "I was going to get a couple hours of sleep and then head back to the hospital."

"May I *kumme*, too?" Trina asked.

"Of course. I'll even show you how to work the reins on the way, if you'd like."

"Don't I need a special license to drive a horse?"

Seth shook his head. "First of all, we don't call it 'driving' a horse. But *neh,* you don't need a special li—" Then he realized she was joking and he smiled until his insides throbbed from the sheer joy of having this *Englischer* as his neighbor.

Epilogue

Usually the convincement process in Willow Creek took at least three or four years, but in Trina's case, she was baptized into the church the following spring, along with several Amish youth. Afterward, there was a special potluck dinner and then Seth took them all home in his buggy. Even though it wasn't raining, he dropped Trina off right at her door before taking Martha and the boys home.

Timothy asked, "Will you watch us ride our bikes in the backyard, *Daed*?" The boys no longer needed training wheels but they were often reckless so Seth preferred they ride on the grass until they gained more control.

"*Neh*, your *daed* has to stable the horse and take care of a few other matters. I'll watch you as long as you don't do any of those *narrish* stunts," Martha said. "Just because Trina bought you helmets to protect your heads doesn't mean you can't break your arm. We can't have that happening again."

She winked at Seth, who shot her a grateful look, knowing she could see his expression. Last year as a Mother's Day present he'd given her the gift of cataract surgery. Although both he and his grandmother had worried about the procedure, Trina and Ethan encouraged them every step of the way. The surgery had been a success; Martha's vision was restored, her headaches vanished and there was no slowing her down now.

There was no slowing Seth down today, either. He stabled his horse and raced next door to see Trina. The silver tabby American shorthair kitten the boys had given her as an honorary Mother's Day gift the previous year had grown into a fourteen-pound cat, thanks in part to Timothy and Tanner constantly supplying it with cream. Named Tabitha by the boys, the cat lounged on the porch railing and flicked her tail as Seth climbed the steps. When she wanted to, Tabitha could be a really good mouser, but apparently, she didn't want to at the moment. Either that, or she'd already completely rid Trina's house of mice.

It seemed to take Trina an eon to open the door after Seth knocked. When she did, he beheld her luminous eyes and was momentarily lost in their beauty, unable to speak. But then language returned to him and he couldn't express himself quickly enough, saying all of the things he'd been prohibited from saying until this moment.

"Trina, I love you. Wholeheartedly and unconditionally, with everything in me, I love you. Not only do I love you, I'm *in* love with you."

"I'm in love with you, too, Seth," she answered, her words tripping over his as if she, too, could no longer contain her emotion. "I always believed in romantic love as a concept, as something necessary for marriage. But until I met you, I never experienced the fullness of being in love. I never experienced—"

But she couldn't finish her sentence because Seth pulled her close and pressed his lips to hers. "You were right," he said breathlessly when they pulled away.

Her eyes were shining. "About what?"

"That was worth the wait." He drew her to him and kissed her again, this time softly and slowly, reluctantly parting only to say, "But I don't ever want to wait that long again."

She put her cheek against his and whispered into his ear, "Ach, the Amish are so impatient."

He could feel her face curling into a smile and he smiled, too.

"Does that mean it's too soon for me to ask if you'll marry me?"

"*Neh*, it's not too soon. Of course I'll marry you!"

They simultaneously tilted their heads and gracefully found each other's lips a third time. Then Seth said, "The *buwe* will be thrilled once we're married and you're living with us. And selling your house should be easy, since you already know a *gut* realtor. Who knows, maybe an *Englisch* family will move in."

"Actually, I was thinking if Martha wants to, she could have my house. It would be like living in a *daadi haus*. She'll have independence and peace and quiet, yet we'll be close enough to give her a hand if she needs it."

"That would be *wunderbaar*. So, when do you want to get married?"

"Well, Amish wedding season is in the fall, so I'd say sometime in late November? Early December?"

"Since I was already married once, technically, we don't have to wait until then. We could get married at any time. We could get married tomorrow, if you want to."

Trina encircled him with her arms. "As

much as I'd love that, I'd actually prefer a traditional Amish fall wedding."

"Okay, if you insist," Seth said with an exaggerated groan to make her laugh. Then he added, "But if you change your mind and want to get married earlier…"

Trina tapped his nose with her fingertip. "I'm not going to change my mind."

"I know. You're always true to your word. It's one of the many things I love about you." There was no longer anything prohibiting them from holding hands, so Seth interlaced his fingers with hers and gently tugged her out onto the porch. "Let's stroll to the creek and on the way I'll tell you some of the other things…"

* * * * *

Dear Reader,

Some characters come to life more easily than others. Seth and Trina's story seemed to flow from my imagination almost as quickly as I could type it. I empathized with Trina as she encountered a different culture and location, and I understood how Seth felt to be in the position of having a new neighbor move in next door. Both situations can be intimidating, awkward and stressful, but they can also provide opportunities for growth, learning and, yes, even love.

I often daydream about what it would be like to live as an Amish person. I admire so many aspects of the Amish lifestyle, especially their emphasis on faith, family and simplicity. (Not to mention their baking abilities!) But I don't think I'd fare well without electricity and modern transportation. So, for now, I'll keep learning about the Amish from books and from my travels.

Thank you for reading the Amish Country Courtships miniseries; there's one more book to come and I hope you'll enjoy it.

Blessings,
Carrie Lighte